RUN, KAT, RUN
MORTALITY BITES SERIES

RAMY VANCE

KEEP EVOLVING STUDIOS

RUN, KAT, RUN

PART I
A BEGINNING OF SORTS:

Humans are idiots.

He should know—he was born a human. And if things continue the way they are, he will die a human.

But he dismisses the thoughts. That will not be his fate—to die human. He will return himself to his former glory.

More so ... he will find the gods and *they* will return him to his former glory.

And that is when he will cease to be a disgusting, worthless human.

And so he sits in the Okinawan airport, scratching at his frail skin that flakes under the weight of his nails, fixated on one thing: a remedy for his current humanity.

The key resides in the hands of one like him ... a former creature of power, rendered human by their departure.

Katrina Darling.

She possesses the final piece of the puzzle he needs to finally leave this plane of existence and follow the gods to their new home.

The final piece of the puzzle he needs so that he can finally cease being human.

He will do anything to make that happen.
And kill anyone who tries to stop him.

AIRPORT SECURITY SUCKS BIGLY

"Raspy Man, I presume?" I kept my voice steady; I didn't want to betray any fear or surprise at seeing him here.

That was harder than expected, because while I'd expected to meet my stalker eventually, the last place I ever expected it to happen was at airport security in Japan. Either this guy had serious clout or mojo, or both ... and that made him way more dangerous than I had previously given him credit for.

He lifted an eyebrow and slightly turned his head in the way one does when trying to process something. "Raspy Man?" Hearing his own voice, he nodded in understanding. "Ahh, I see. I have had many names, but such a nom de plume has never been among them. Given the factitious nature in which you've thus dubbed me, I do not care for it. Call me Tomás. Of all my human names, that one was my favorite. It was when I felt most productive."

He pronounced his name in that pretentious way Europeans did, and I heard a hint of Catalonia in his accent. But not present-day Catalonia ... I'm talking hundreds-of-years-ago twang.

A playful lip curled, and I saw a man who, although he had the voice of a lifetime smoker, was actually quite handsome. Solid jaw, deep-set eyes that betrayed great wisdom, smooth skin and a demeanor that screamed infinite confidence.

Granted, he was older—probably mid-fifties—and bald, but he possessed a Bruce Willis-esque rugged handsomeness. He also had a huge scar around his neck, like someone had tried to simultaneously hang him while slashing his throat. And recently, too. I've been around enough scars to know that one was less than a decade old. Maybe only a few years, at that.

Still, as far as scars went, this one was all kinds of sexy.

I shook my head. *"Now's not the time to develop a crush on your stalker,"* I thought, but then I looked up at eyes that promised me salvation. *"Then again ..."* I mused.

He chuckled at this. "I heard about your proclivities for audible thinking. I was told that this particular quirk was extremely ..." He paused as he thought of the word. "Grating."

"Hey," I said in mock-offense.

He lifted a placating hand. "But given the nature of your thoughts, I must say that my sources are incorrect. Rare for them, really." He gave me a sly smile that made my heart flutter.

And even though I found myself attracted to this man, the whole situation was beyond ridiculous. I mean, I was literally in a Japanese airport, sitting before a man of European descent that somehow ... what? Bribed airport security to get a private meeting with me?

Which becomes supercalifragillistically ridiculous when you put into context that all this comes on the heels of having slain not one, not two, but *three* gods after averting an interspecies war.

I started to laugh. Given the speed with which his smile disappeared, I knew my reaction was the last thing he expected. "Let me guess," I said. "That slicker-than-slick smile? Something you spent years practicing. It's what, Raspy Man's version of Joey's 'How you doing?' " I put on a fake Italian accent as I mocked the *Friends* catchphrase.

If Raspy Man was offended by laughter, it was short-lived, because he started to laugh, too. "Indeed," he said. "Centuries of practice, and I must admit that you are the first human female"—he paused—"or *male* to react with laughter."

"Let me guess. They swooned and fell in your arms."

"More like they fell to their knees."

Yuck, that got R-rated way too quickly. "How eloquent," I said, "I see all your centuries has made you just another man who is obsessed with his junk."

He sighed, seeing his faux pas. But from the way he carried himself, he wasn't too concerned by it, either. "The truth rarely is," he said. "I find eloquence is best delegated to situations that require finesse, manipulation and lies. And Ms. Darling, I respect you far too much to attempt any of those shenanigans with you. Now, after our business is concluded, perhaps we can explore such things ..." He let the words hang, and I knew he was serious. After our business was concluded, he'd happily explore something a little less businessy with me.

And why not? I was cute as a button and sexy to boot.

But he'd come here for a reason—orchestrated our meeting for the sole purpose of finding out what had happened to his soul. It took every ounce of my will, honed by centuries of bluffing, not to touch the hugely magical, itsy-bitsy Soul Jar hanging around my neck.

As far as I knew, the Soul Jar possessed his soul. But what was farther from what I knew—as in, *another planet away* farther—was how trustworthy this guy was. After all, I'd literally died getting this thing, and I wasn't about to hand it over to someone I wasn't 100% sure wasn't evil.

And this guy definitely had James Bond villain written all over him. All he needed to do was creepily stroke a cat and the image would be complete.

"I'm not much of an explorer," I said. "Besides, I have a boyfriend."

"Ahh, yes. The AlwaysMortal Justin Truly. As a boy toy, yes. But is there really much of a future for you two? After all, he is off gallivanting with another."

He paused to scan my expression. Even though the thought that

Justin would be cheating on me stung, I also didn't believe this asshole. He was trying to rattle me, catch me off guard and—

Raspy Man picked up his briefcase and opened it on the table. Inside was all kinds of packaging, with tons of what looked like contact lens cases in it. There was also a ... what the hell was that? A crystal ball?

As in the cliché, I'm-in-an-episode-of-*Charmed* crystal ball. "Or at least, he will be two weeks from now. Look for yourself." Picking up the crystal ball, he tapped it and, sure enough, images of Justin popped up. In it, I saw Justin hugging a redheaded, pale-skinned girl who looked way, way too pretty for my liking.

Having this guy try to throw me off guard with a statement was one thing, but seeing photographic evidence was another thing altogether. I pursed my lips. *Come on, Kat, this could very well be a life-and-death situation. No point in getting all jealous now. Save that for when you're not sitting across ... across from whatever he is,* I thought (in my head).

Because no matter what Justin was or was not doing, those photos proved one thing: Raspy Man was having him followed. If I showed that I cared about him, that could lead to another kidnapping, or worse. And as pissed off as I was at him, he didn't deserve to die because of me.

I considered going the *"How can I trust you, or this thing?"* route. After all, it could be an illusion, and this thing could be the celestial equivalent of Photoshop. Something witty like that.

But that would betray that I cared for Justin. I needed to make sure he'd be safe, so I went with the best course of action when a psychopath is threatening your boyfriend.

"Fine." I pushed the ball away from me. "He's cheating. Or he will be cheating. So what?" If you're going to lie convincingly, you've got to believe it yourself. So I did my best to believe what I was saying. Which was easier than I thought.

Raspy Man was a bit surprised by my reaction, but that surprise was quickly supplanted by a smile as he gave me enthusiastic applause. "Truth is elusive. And after centuries of living, you and I

8

both know there are many truths to everything. I see you've found one that you believe is best. And your delivery ... nearly perfect. You would have fooled any human, and most immortals"—he paused at the word *immortals*, before adding—"*Once*Immortals, I mean. Very good."

He returned the crystal ball to the case before leaning in, bridging the divide of the desk between us. "How about we say this: Justin is off limits. I'll even go as far as to promise that no AlwaysMortal you care about will be touched: Justin, Aimee, Bogdan ... even the very aged Cassandra. Although technically not an AlwaysMortal, I will happily extend this amnesty to her as well. What do you say?"

I nodded. "Great, but your statement also implies that others—or rather, the *Others* I care about—are fair game. And that statement further implies that you're not a nice guy."

"We are not!" he said, the words booming out of him in a momentary lack of self-control. He cleared his throat before repeating in a gentler tone, "We are not ... nice. Kind. Pleasant. We are beyond such concepts. Certainly centuries of feeding on them has proven that to you."

"So what, you're an ex-vamp, too?" I pretended to be bored. "I figured, but wasn't sure. After all, you could have been an ex-werewolf or ex-were—"

"No, my dear. I was never a vampire. I was something much, much worse."

↔

"But you have fangy creature of the night written all over you," I said, somewhat surprised he wasn't an ex-vamp.

At this, he chuckled. "I enjoy the sun far too much to allow myself such a debilitating defect."

Allow? Defect? Who the hell is this guy?

He gave me a hard stare, locking his gray eyes with my baby blues, and whereas initially I was all like, *Eww, old guy ogling*, I found that I was very quickly falling into his gaze. I don't mean it in the we-locked-eyes-and-something-inside-me-went-all-gooey-and-soft way. I mean that I was actually drawn into them. It was like being pulled in by an invisible force like gravity, or ... or ...

"Magic," I whispered.

Hearing my own voice was enough to jar me out of whatever spell he was casting, and I closed my eyes before shaking my head.

He was playing with me.

Hell-l-l-l-l no!

After centuries of being the one who *played* with my prey, the last thing I would ever tolerate was assuming the role of the toy. I considered it a matter of professional pride.

"A charm spell, to be specific," I said, scanning his face for any signs of aging. I had near perfect memory and the ability to take snapshots of things—not a vampire thing, just one of my God-given gifts (well, GoneGod-given, at least).

I had taken a snapshot of him when we entered, and comparing that image with how he looked now, I saw that he hadn't aged at all.

"So, no aging." I looked around the sparse room. "And given you just tried some version of a charm spell, you're using a magical item. Something imbued with magic before the gods left. But what could it be ... What could it be?"

Nothing stood out as obvious, so either he was hiding the item, or ... "Holy guacamole," I muttered, leaning in close to get a better look at his eyes. They were blue with shifting nimbuses of gray, like a lone storm cloud in an otherwise clear sky. "The magic is coming from your eyes. Like Cassandra. Those aren't the eyes you were born with, are they?"

The strange man laughed. I mean, genuinely laughed. And given how destroyed his throat was, it came out like an old Volkswagen backfiring. He clapped his hands as he did, and even though I could tell this was his version of keeling over and chortling ... he still managed to do it in a somewhat reserved manner. "Ever since the gods left, I have been looking for someone like you."

"What, someone button-cute to stalk?"

"No, Katrina—a mate. A mate to share this horrible GoneGod World with …"

2
MOST AWKWARD MARRIAGE
PROPOSAL EVER

"*E*xcuse me?" I said.

"Come now, you must admit that this new world is lonely. So many lost, damned souls. So many lesser beings to share space with," he said. "The thought of finding someone worthy"—he laid his hand on the briefcase holding the crystal ball he had used to show me Justin—"someone who understands who we are … You, too, must be looking for an appropriate partner."

"Partner?" I narrowed my eyes. "You must really think highly of yourself if you think that … that … whatever *that* was would make me all weak at the knees."

"No, of course not. Our relationship is just beginning. You have yet to see my worth. Still …" He touched the inside of his left eye like someone removing a contact lens. And as he moved his finger, I saw that was exactly what he was doing.

A thin film rested on his finger and, with his other hand, he picked up his briefcase and opened it. Inside were several of those mini-pods. Picking up a lone case, he put the film inside and slid it over to me.

"A gift. Part of my dowry, let's say."

"There are a bunch of problems with this, but because I really want to catch my flight, I'm only going to highlight the top three," I said. "A, dowries are so last century. We modern girls prefer less possessive gestures. B, I'm not marrying you. And let me make my reasoning perfectly clear: it's not me ... it's you. And C—and believe me when I say that this is the clincher—giving a girl a discarded contact lens is a poor substitute for a bouquet of flowers. It's all kinds of gross. You really need to work on your game."

Another smile. "In the centuries to come, I will enjoy your wit."

"Centuries? I'm not sure if you got the memo, but we're all mortal now."

He ignored me, casually pointing at the case like he was pointing at some worthless trinket. "That discarded lens, as you call it, is the pared cornea of the Goddess Turan. That filament does not simply charm, as you put it. It stirs one's inner desires—enflames them, if you will. And that is my gift to you."

"Goddess? How the hell did this guy get a goddess's eye?"

"It was a gift," he said, pulling out another lens, "in exchange for certain ... services rendered."

Damn it! I must have been speaking out loud again. Note to self: out loud thinking bad thing to do when in life-and-death situation. Still, the way he answered the question was quite specific. The word *rendered* can mean 'service provided or given,' but it can also mean 'to become.' And given how deliberate he was about the word, I figured he hadn't chosen it lightly. I wanted to know more. Hell, if I was going to beat him, I needed to know more.

"Rendered?" I drew out the word. "What exactly does 'render' mean?"

He gave me a disappointed look that said I should know *exactly* what he meant. "Katrina"—he wagged a condescending finger in my direction—"I understand that you've spent most of your time on this Earth as a common vampire. But still, I see a curious mind within. Surely your travels must shed some light on how the gods used me."

"Patronizing much?"

"Only when necessary."

He tapped his finger against the table three times as he debated telling me. I figured I'd tip the scales in my favor with a wee bit of what centuries of life had taught me again and again: men are easily distracted. Playing with my blouse's top button in a nervous manner, I bit my lower lip before saying, "I want to understand" in the same voice I once convinced my would-be executioner to let me out during a brief stint in a Victorian dungeon.

His eyes were drawn to my fingers, then my lips, and as soon as my words hit his ears, he nodded. "Good. You're at least trying to gain the upper hand. That deserves a reward, don't you think?"

So much for that. Still ... I was getting somewhere.

I gestured for him to go on.

"Very well." He lifted his briefcase again and opened it. Inside, dozens of contact lens cases still sat in their spongy-foam protective casing. Singles and doubles, with seven of the foam holes empty. And given that he was a bespoke kind of guy, I figured one was in his right eye, one was on the table and the other five were ... where? Lost? In some henchman's eye? I'd have to err on the side of caution and go with eye-modified super henchman.

He picked up two lenses. "From Ra." Then two more. "And these were a gift from the Incan goddess Inti. These are from Brovo and this one"—he picked up a single casing and held it between his fingers in a not-unlike-Gollum-and-the-Ring-fashion—"this one is the prize of my collection. Odin's eye—the missing eye—collected just after he sacrificed it in the Well of Urd. Great wisdom is revealed when I gaze upon this world through its lens and—"

I stretched out my arms and gave Raspy Man an exaggerated yawn.

"I'm sorry," he said, genuinely surprised. "Are you bored?"

"You know," I said, wagging a condescending finger of my own, "you might have ignored my little finger-on-the-button technique and my *Excuse me mister, but can you help me?* lip bite, but at the end of the day, you're just like every other guy who likes to drone on about his hobby. On and on and on ... If I was interested in sleeping with you, I'd be all like, 'That's interesting.' " I put a hand on my not-insubstantial chest. " 'Please tell me more. You are so fascinating.' But I'm not interested. As in, at all. So let's skip all this preamble and get straight to the 'rendering.' And please focus this time."

Truth was, I was fascinated. But being fascinated by this guy wasn't going to help with my bigger life goals ... which at this moment was one of survival.

Raspy Man gave me a curious look before letting out another bellow of laughter. "You, my dear, shall be a fountain of amusement in the centuries to come."

Again with that word, *centuries*. Like he was in total denial that we were all going to die—and if he kept being a patronizing asshole, from me stabbing him rather than old age.

"Very well." He pulled out a handkerchief and dabbed the corner of his left eye. "I shall provide you with the promised explanation."

He took a deep breath, and as he let it out, all mirth and humor left him. "The gods have always needed help speaking to humans because" —he gestured in the general direction of outside, clearly denoting both he and I were not human—"whenever the gods *did* speak to them, humans tended to go insane."

"Are you getting H.P. Lovecraftian on me?"

"Prime example," he said. "Although he held his mind together better than most. And he was smart enough to not use the gods' real names, instead making them up—C'thalpa, Cthulhu and my personal favorite, the Cloud Thing, which was really just a drunk Cupid messing with the poor man. But, before I receive another yawn, allow me to get back on point."

"Please do."

"Only certain beings could speak to the gods, and only under certain circumstances. I was one of those beings ... a creation who moved through the ages, speaking on behalf of the gods."

"So what are you saying?" I leaned forward. "You were a professional prophet, spreading the good word in various guises?"

"Oh please. Do not think so little of me."

"What, you're offended that I called you a prophet?"

"Prophets are human. I am nothing so debased."

"But you're human now."

"Indeed." He laced the word with genuine frustration.

"So ..." I gestured for him to finish the thought.

"So what?"

"So if you're human now, that means you were born a human. That's what happened when the gods left. Vampires, werewolves, zombies—they all reverted back to their human selves. Given that you are human now, that means you were born a human. And judging by how forlorn you are, I'm guessing that was a long, long, long time ago."

He nodded. "Indeed."

"So why all the hatred toward humans? I mean, I spent three hundred years as a vampire and now that I'm human again, I'm really trying to make a go of it. You, on the other hand, are all 'Bah, humbug' about it."

He paused, considering my question. When he did answer, it was no knee-jerk reaction, and what he said next stilled my blood with fear.

"Because, unlike you, I didn't spend my time here on Earth amongst the other humans. At least, not all of it. Most of my time was spent ... elsewhere."

"OK, I'll bite. Where did you spend it?"

"Why, in Heaven, my dear. By God's side."

3
THE MOST POWERFUL
HUMAN EVER

"*H*oly shit," I whispered in unabashed awe. And then it hit me exactly who this guy was. I mean, how could I not know? I spend my formative years as a young, faithful Christian girl in Inverness. Pretty much the only reading available was the Bible, and Sunday church was 90% of my socialization.

"You …" I stammered. "You're Enoch, aren't you?"

Raspy Man gave me an appreciative smile. "Now that is the Katrina Darling I have been longing to meet. Smart, deductive and reverent. I do not approve of your use of language." He stood up and ran his hands over his head before adding, "Then let us drop the façade. I am Enoch."

"So if you're Enoch, why use the name Tomás, then?"

"Enoch is a … complicated name known and feared by many. Not your average human, mind you. But to your average Other … that is another story. So I borrowed the name Tomás from a man I used long ago when I was trying to set things right. Tomás de Torquemada was one of the greatest Inquisitors and a true man of faith. He was one of the few humans I could converse with without all the drooling insanity that usually followed." He chuckled at his little joke.

Not that I heard any of it. I was sitting in front of Enoch. Enoch the prophet ... the one whom God had plucked from Earth and transformed into the Archangel Metatron (not to be confused with Megatron from *Transformers* ... Although, given this guy was transformed, the similarities were undeniable).

Few people know this, but the three most important people in the Bible, in descending order, are Jesus, Isaiah and Enoch. Why? Because all three did not die when they were taken to Heaven. Granted, Jesus was a bit of a special case, but still ...

What's more, this guy had two whole Biblical texts named after him. Of course, neither text was canonized or official doctrine, but I had lived long enough to know that so much that really happened was never officially recognized as true.

And seeing this man before me, I figured the stories about him must be true. Here was the human hand-picked by God to become an archangel so that he could witness ... well ... everything.

According to both canonized texts and the ones never officially recognized, Enoch was in the prime of his life when he was enlisted by God to help judge the angels who were doing all sorts of nasty stuff on Earth. Fornicating, teaching humans stuff they shouldn't know ... fornicating some more.

"When the gods left," Enoch continued, "they did not take me like the other prophets. They cast me down here, in this form." He balled his hands into fists as if experimenting with his "new" body. "They made me less, and why?"

"Because you never died."

"Indeed. I never died. An angel with a soul, and since they couldn't separate my soul from my body, I was left behind."

"Is that how you got that?" I gestured to the slit across his neck.

Enoch nodded. "I knew the gods were leaving. I was, after all, witness to their plans. I also knew that they meant to leave me behind. So the moment the gods departed—the moment I was transformed into my human form—I sought to end my life so that my soul could join them."

"But instead of your soul getting a one-way ticket out of here, it got trapped in the Soul Jar?"

He shook his head. "That came later. No, I'm afraid that my attempts to end my own life were foiled by …" He paused, shaking his head again. "Let us just leave it at foiled … for now."

"How 1970s action-movie-villain-y of you."

Enoch shrugged. "Like I said, we have centuries to speak. I will tell you all in due time."

"You keep saying that—centuries—but we're going to die. You know that, right? We've got a few good decades in us and that's it. Then it's bye bye birdie for us."

"Perhaps. But with the Soul Jar, we may circumvent the limitations of our mortality."

"How? By becoming vampires again? My mom already tried that and—"

"I'm afraid that was the lie I told your mother to get her to find the … what do you call it? The Soul Jar?" He pulled another lens out of the case. "But the endgame was never to become a vampire, or any other kind of immortal creature."

"Then what's the plan?"

He popped in the fresh lens and stared at me with his new eye from GoneGod knows which Other or god he took it from. "Why, to follow the gods to their new plane of existence, of course."

He closed his eyes like he was preparing himself for what would come next. I'd seen that kind of prep work before. Hell, it was something I did every time I was about to enter an intense training session. Whatever that particular eye did, it was going to hurt him. A lot.

"Wait," I said. "Before you do whatever you're about to do, answer me this. Why do you keep saying 'we?' Like I don't have a choice but to follow you."

"There is always a choice."

"But you assume I'll go with you. Why?"

"Because I will offer you safe passage."

"Safe passage?"

"To follow the gods. But to do so … Well, there is only one way to follow the them to their new home, and doing so requires not only great magic but also great resolve and sacrifice."

"I take it that when you say 'sacrifice,' you don't mean sacrificing pizza for boiled chicken."

He chuckled, his eyes still closed. "Again, indeed. Now let us get to the business at hand." He slowly opened his eyes. "My soul, and its whereabouts."

↔

As he stared at me, I realized that I was sunk. Unlike the last eye that gave his retina a gray halo, this one turned it into an unnatural purple. Which was particularly jarring, given that his other eye was more of a subtle gray-blue. So this one did something different. But what?

I had no idea what that eye did, because if he had an eye that could stir one's inner desires, who knows what that one could do? A human (and Other) lie detector? Or perhaps it would compel me to tell the truth? Another charm spell?

I focused on myself to see if my will or desires were being pulled one way or another. I felt nothing. No inner stirring, no *So unlike you, Kat* desires or needs. I was just me. Of that I was sure. After all, I had centuries of being me.

So, no mojo going on here? Right?

"*Shit*," I thought—out loud. "What's the game?"

But he didn't say anything. He just continued to stare at me with that creepy eye.

In my three hundred years, I've been in this kind of situation more times then I care to count. OK, that's a wee bit of a lie … I've never been in this type of situation—Raspy Man was all kinds of weird—but I have been in front of diabolical masterminds hell-bent on something evil that usually included *Kill Kat* on their to-do list.

So I did what I always do when put in this situation.

I ran.

Very hero-like, might I add.

4
RUN, KAT, RUN

I put both hands on the table and hoisted with all my might. I don't know what it was about this guy. Maybe it was all the talk about immortality and stuff, but I think I forgot I was human, because I expected to be able to throw the metal table against the wall, flattening him with it as a bonus.

Instead, my human strength barely managed to tip it before its legs came crashing back to the ground.

Great ... so much for my dramatic exit. I only managed to move the table a couple inches, inconveniencing him not at all.

"Come now, Kat. Do you really think such dramatics are necessary?" He was still scanning me. His eyes rested on my reasonably substantial chest and they widened.

A bit of a dramatic response, given I was wearing a blouse that showed practically no cleavage. Which meant that he wasn't looking at my boobs ... He was staring at the pendant hanging under my shirt. The Soul Jar. Shit, I should have given the damn thing to Deirdre.

"So you do have it," he said, his voice a whisper.

Shit, shit, shit ... "Shit!" I said, considering my next move. The table might have been too heavy to lift, but not everything in this room was made of sturdy metal.

I grabbed the chair I sat on, and with one graceful pivot that would have made a golfer green with envy, clocked him on the head with it.

He went down, which was the only reassuring thing about our whole exchange. That, and the fact that the chair's leg caused him to bleed red. As in, human-blood red.

Whatever this guy was, he was human. Right now, at least.

I didn't wait for him to get up and do whatever evil geniuses did when knocked over by a five-foot-nothing, hundred-and-one-pounds-of-kick-ass-dynamite did.

Heading for the door, I ran.

↔

The Okinawan airport was surprisingly big, given it was built for such a tiny island. But it was a resort area—the Hawaii of Japan—and thousands of tourists visited the archipelago every year. And I was in its bowels, the back rooms purposely placed out of the way so that any escaping prisoners, like little ol' *moi*, wouldn't terrify the tourists.

Plus, I was a terribly cute, auburn *gaijin* girl running out of one of those out-of-the-way rooms. I stuck out like a sore yara-mah-ya-who (a bright-red, thumb-like creature, for the uninitiated). I tried to act cool as I hurried through the corridors, but I didn't get five steps before someone from Japanese airport security put a hand on my shoulder. *"Chotomatte-kudasai."* One minute, please.

Even in a chase scene, Japanese were polite.

I lifted a wagging finger, and forcing out fake tears I'd used more than once as a vampire when luring in unsuspecting prey, cried, *"Sca'bei."* Pervert.

I pointed at the door that I had just exited. My hope was that the guard would assume I had been assaulted by Tomás, and his righteous indignation would distract him enough for me to keep running.

Great plan ... And to accentuate my claim, out came the bleeding Tomás. Thank the GoneGods for perfect timing. Things were going my way.

Except the guard only looked at Tomás, his eyes widening in shock as he cried out, *"Torukumada-sama."*

Sama. A term of respect in Japanese culture. So much for the man of the law protecting innocent little me.

The guard's hand tightened on my shoulder, and seeing that he meant to subdue me, I sent a roundhouse kick into his stomach, knocking the wind out of him with a satisfying *oof.*

The guard went down, releasing me. And although I was free of his grip, I saw dozens of shocked eyes look over at me.

I think this is where the expression "Out of the frying pan and into the fire" comes from.

↔

Literally the only thing I had going for me was the fact that Japanese police do not carry guns. What wasn't going in my favor was the terrifying fact that most police were extensively trained in the martial arts —specifically, aikido.

Which meant they were experts at subduing. And grappling. And generally incapacitating.

Turning on my heels, I ran in the direction I had come from.

Two guards tried to stop me, and using a technique I had learned from multiple martial arts masters through the ages, I kicked the first guy in the balls before dropping to one knee and punching the next one in the exact same spot.

Sometimes I wonder why the gods gave them such an obvious weakness.

They both fell to their knees, and I ran past them and into the main area of the airport. Ahead of me I could see the doors to the outside. I just had to get through security—in the opposite direction as was intended—and out the door.

I ran to the baggage x-rays, where a female guard with a baton swung at me. Seeing that her anatomy didn't allow for the same trick, I ducked under her swing and kicked her in the shins. She went down with a yelp, but recovered with surprising quickness as she swung her baton, cracking me on the shoulder.

"Oww," I said. It took every ounce of my will to *not* curl into the fetal position and whimper.

She might have been trained in aikido, but so was I … and I had centuries to practice it, too. Using a fairly common wrist technique, I managed to get the baton out of her hands and knock it to the ground, where I was able to pick it up.

I crashed through the human metal detectors, which rang with baton-inspired alarm. Two more guards charged at me, and I could see several police gathering at the front entrance.

Escaping a place with so much coordinated security wasn't going to happen. Not without a miracle. And those disappeared the day the gods left.

Seeing that I was beat, I got to my knees, dropped the baton and lifted my hands up in surrender.

At least this way, I might escape any beatings from more batons.

But not all the miracles were taken, it seemed. There were still a couple around. And a miracle came swooping in, grabbing the two security guards that had been descending on me and throwing them both at the baggage x-ray with an alarm-beeping crash.

A hand hoisted me to my feet as a concerned voice uttered, "Milady. Did they harm you?"

Deirdre. My fae miracle incarnate.

5

AIRPORT SECURITY REALLY SUCKS

*D*eirdre offered me a hand and said in a completely unfastidious, deadpan manner, "Come with me if you want to live."

I had known my fae warrior friend long enough to understand that she had never seen any of the *Terminator* series, nor understood the joke. She was serious—as in, deadly so.

I took her hand.

She hoisted me to my feet with an effortless pull and turned to face several guards who had appeared on the scene. As far as I could tell, they were all human, normal-looking Japanese security. None of them had a Raspy-Man's-henchmen vibe to them.

"They're civilians," I said.

Deirdre nodded in understanding. "Hospitalization only. I understand."

I groaned. I'd preferred that no one got hurt, but the reality was you didn't escape an airport without someone getting hurt. My only hope was that anything the fae warrior broke would be mendable with modern medicine.

Three male guards charged at us, and Deirdre picked up one of the metal tables used to repack your stuff after the x-ray. It was bolted to the ground—not that it mattered to her.

With a single pivot that made my chair-golf-swing from earlier look positively amateurish, she swung it at the guards, sending them flying. None of them looked too hurt (thank the GoneGods for small miracles).

But after that little display of power, none of the other guards dared charge at her. Instead, they tried to form a human shield of sorts, preventing our exit. They were buying time, and given the current state of affairs, I knew what their play was.

They were waiting for some of the anti-Other weaponry to appear on the scene. Since the Others arrived, so had a whole new industry centered on Other-defensive weapons. Nets for valkyrie and angels, supercharged cattle-prods for minotaurs and centaurs, and souped-up tranquilizers for just about everyone else.

We needed out, and we needed out now.

Deirdre knew it too, because without asking, my little fae warrior did something that hurt me in unfixable ways. She picked me up like a football and—quite literally—ran me through and onto the other side of security and out of the airport.

The sun hit a relatively unbruised, unhurt body ... but my ego? Boy oh boy, my ego ached.

↔

Outside, I scanned the area for our next move. I was considering ... ahem ... "borrowing" a car conveniently left by one of the many drop-offs that were happening.

My attention was caught by a red Toyota I had never seen before (probably a Japanese-only product). It looked fast. And best of all, it already had Egya in the driver's seat. Go team!

"Here I am again, thinking and saving. Saving and thinking." Egya leaned over and opened the passenger-side door. "Your chariot awaits."

"Yeah … thanks," I said, mentally groaning. Egya was going to lord this one over me for months to come. "Come on, Deirdre," I said. "Let's get out of here."

Deirdre didn't move.

"Come on, girl. We got an out," I repeated.

But the fae warrior didn't move, her back to the road as she diligently watched the insides of the airport. She was quite literally watching my back.

"Deirdre," I said, urgency in my voice. "Now!" I turned to see that, whereas the fae warrior *was* facing the airport, she wasn't watching anything. She was frozen, her face void of all expression as her arms hung limp at her sides.

"What the—" I started when Enoch walked outside. He held what looked like a silver coin the size of a tea plate in his hand, and I would have dismissed it as such except for the rune on its surface.

"The Celtic god, Alator, knew that his creations were particularly willful," he rasped, strolling out of the airport like he had all the time in the world.

Not only did he stroll out like he wasn't in the middle of a fight, but no one else exited the airport with him. No security, no henchmen … Hell, there weren't even any tourists or travelers. No one.

That isn't to say that no one was around. A family was hugging goodbye not ten feet from where we stood. Another couple bickered within earshot. Meanwhile, a taxi drove up and let out a woman with way too little luggage to be travelling anywhere far. She strolled right past us like we didn't exist.

Hell, I could even see an Okinawan security guard pacing on the other side of a sliding door.

This guy must have cast some serious mojo on this place to hide us like that. He was one seriously souped-up villain. But that wasn't what scared me the most.

He was alone because he wanted to be alone.

And he was completely unafraid. Which meant that either he was overconfident ... or he knew without a shadow of a doubt that we posed no threat.

"You see, elves, halflings, changelings—all of the fae," he rasped, "they possess great power and even greater passion. For unlike most Others, they were built on the principle of love. And love, as you well know, makes us do very silly things." Then, as if contemplating something esoteric, added, "In many ways, I believe that the fae are humans' closest cousin. Evolutionarily speaking."

He chuckled at his own joke, which given his condition, sounded more like a flooded engine turning over.

"Whether I am right or not, there is no denying that the fae, like humans, are oft led astray by their principles. So Alator knew it to be inevitable that, from time to time, a few upstarts would challenge his dominion. That is why he created this."

He lifted the silver disk to the middle of his chest, and with every inch that stone rose, Deirdre lowered herself until she was on her knees.

"No fae can resist this spell, with this side subduing the upstart. And as for this side ..." He turned the coin, revealing another rune. This one looked like a child's drawing of a tent with stick-figure people hovering above. As soon as Deirdre saw it, she stood up, clenching her fists. "Subservience."

"Deirdre," I said, trying to get her to move. But dragging a changeling who didn't want to be dragged was like trying to drag a mountain. Deirdre didn't even budge.

Enoch looked at the kneeling fae. "My dear changeling," he whispered, "bring me the Kat."

Without hesitation or warning, Deirdre turned on me, grappling me into submission and squeezing.

↔

Egya. I knew my Ghanaian friend was lurking in the background. He was an accomplished hunter and warrior. In our first true battle together, he managed to remove a magic ring that controlled a troop of mindless (but very powerful) jinn creatures. He did it by cutting off that Big Bad's finger.

I figured he had something similar up his sleeve. And all I needed to do was serve as a distraction. "Let me go," I said in as helpless a voice as I could muster. "Please." With that word, I managed to squeeze out a few tears.

"Crying, Katrina? That is so unlike you."

"Yeah, well, you didn't just have to fight three dead gods. That's after losing your soul *after* regaining it and becoming human again. An event that, might I add, took place while I was in the middle of feeding. Feeding as a vampire." I put in as much confusion and pain as I could, going for the frantic, out-of-control-crying approach. I figured that if this guy really wanted to marry me, then seeing me like this was bound to raise an eyebrow. And, if I was really lucky, some empathy.

As I continued my barely coherent, tear-filled rant, I was surprised by how easy it all came out. I mean, I had wanted to do it as a rouse, a distraction so Egya could get into position, but this … this hit home far more closely than I'd expected.

What can I say? Mortality truly does bite.

"And to top it all off," I finally let out, "my best friend has betrayed me for you, and all because you have the gods' greatest hits on DVD in your hand."

As soon as those words left my lips, Egya sprang from behind Enoch. He had a knife and was going for the former archangel's hand. Any second now and this guy would lose a finger, drop the disk and then it would be my turn to subdue.

With a couple fists in his face.

But Egya's blade paused about three millimeters from Enoch's thumb. The Ghanaian hunter was frozen in an awkward crouching position. I had no idea what magic Enoch was using this time.

Another contact lens? A shiny disk hidden somewhere? For all I knew, he had paralyzing sunscreen on his bald head.

"Ahh, the were-hyena comes out to play." Enoch didn't even look down at him. "You can stop your babbling now. As you can see, I am not so easily distracted."

My face went cold. "Apparently not."

Enoch tilted his head. "Much better. Now, what should I do? I could slit his throat. He wouldn't move while bleeding out—his body would go into rigor mortis in that position. Or I could just leave him thus, forever."

"Well, that might be his preference. After all, he does do yoga."

Enoch chuckled. "Gallows humor. Endearing." Then he shrugged like a parent giving in to his toddler's demands. "You do love the boy, so killing him would put a permanent black mark on our upcoming nuptials. Instead, I shall offer him as a gift to you. Your very first pet."

And with a wave of his hand, I watched in horror as Egya's body contorted and writhed, turning into a hyena before my very eyes.

6

FAE SLAVES AND PET HYENAS

I once saw a hyena at a zoo. They were lanky canines with a hedgehog-like mane and a permanent resting I-know-something-you-don't-and-it's-hilarious face. They were also quite small, not much larger than an average-sized labrador.

Egya, on the other hand, was huge—easily the size of, well, the six-foot-nothing, muscular young man that he was. Unlike other hyenas I've seen, he wasn't brown, either, but black as night with pearly white teeth. Also, his mouth carried the same mischievous, half-cocked smile that he always wore, and I knew he was still in there.

"Oh great," I said. "He was annoying enough as a human. But now he's going to shed, too."

Enoch chuckled. And so did Egya, his hyena lips pulling back in that way they did whenever he found something really funny.

"It's good to see you're still in there," I said. "And as for you, Mr. I-Was-An-Angel-and-Now-I'm-Not … what's the plan?"

"The Soul Jar." He put out his hand.

"And what? I hand it over and you'll let us go?"

Enoch's lips curled. "I wouldn't be—how did you put it?—the Big Bad if I did. No, I will not let you go, but I also promise not to kill your pet."

He placed a hand on Egya's scruff and the damn overgrown canine just sat down. I mean, he literally just sat down. Like a good dog.

Crap.

Enoch had some mojo going on with him, too.

So, let's assess. In the span of ten minutes, Enoch had managed to charm both my best friends, using them against me. One of them ended up sitting before him, prone, and probably wouldn't move a muscle while Enoch broke his neck.

The other said best friend had me in a grip that made Hulk Hogan's signature move seem like a hug. (What? Not a WWF wrestling fan from the 1980s? Google it. Trust me, you missed out.) Annnnd ... he had enough of a magical arsenal on him to literally make this entire airport do his bidding.

And what did I have going for me? He seemed to have an, ahem, interest in fornicating with me. I could try to seduce him, but my weak-and-helpless tack had failed. Somehow I don't think my *Oh my, you are so powerful and handsome that I am suddenly overcome with lust* routine would work, either.

Besides, from what I could tell, he wasn't interested in possessing me. He actually wanted me to want him.

Otherwise he wouldn't have given me that gooey contact lens and—

"OK," I said. "OK, I get it."

Enoch lifted a curious eyebrow.

"I get your awkward proposal—your plan to destroy the world and your desire to take me with you."

"Enlighten me." He folded his arms over his chest. At least he didn't have a menacing hand on Egya's scruff.

"You were Enoch. Then you were Metatron, the Witness."

He feigned a yawn. "We've been over this, Darling. If this is some kind of stalling technique, don't bother. My spells will last for as long as I need them to. We could literally stand here until we're old and gray, and no one would come to save you."

"I know, I know. You've made it perfectly clear that you're in charge. But that's just the thing: you're in charge. And that's the problem, isn't it?"

He tilted his head, an appreciative smile crawling across his face. "And?"

"And that's a problem for you … sort of." I paused. He was impressed, which meant he was curious. And I'd played the captor-captive game enough times to know that meant I had leverage.

I waited for him to speak. But he didn't. Not for a long time. Instead, he just stared at me like he was trying to unravel a puzzle. *Good luck, buddy. Tons of guys have tried to figure out this puzzle,* I thought (in my head. Hey, I might have a weird quirk, but even I can control it in life-and-death situations … most of the time).

Just when I thought he was never going to speak again, he nodded, the debate in his head evidently over. "Deirdre, my fae warrior, please let Kat go. But do be so kind as to keep a hand on her shoulder, should she try … well, anything."

Now it was my turn to stand dumbfounded.

"What?" he rasped. "Isn't that what you wanted? To use my curiosity to procure your release? Well, there you have it—you are free of her grasp." He gave me one of those slow, mocking claps.

An Other who got sarcasm. He was going to be a formidable foe.

"Yeah, fine. But no lies, right? Isn't that what you said? Tell me: just now, were you reading my mind?"

Enoch narrowed his eyes. "Yes and no."

"That's not an answer."

"It is also not a lie."

"Not answering is lying by omission," was something my mother always said. And look at me now, using her annoyingness to my advantage.

"Humph, very well. As you mentioned, I was the Witness for eons, observing thousands before me. Granted, most of my observations were of angels and gods and powerful Others. My experience with humans is limited. But you are not a human. Not anymore, at least."

I didn't want to get into a debate with him about the meaning of humanity and my desire to renew my membership. Instead, I just conceded his point with a nod. *No lies, remember?*

"So now that your little gambit of silence has paid off ... continue."

"You were an angel. And angels all have their 'thing,' right? Michael is the Protector. Even after the gods left, that's his thing. A thing he chose to fulfill by being a cop in Paradise Lot." As I said the archangel's name, I wondered if I'd ever be able to get to Paradise Lot and fulfill Gabriel's request. "Penemue knows all that is written. Miral is the Angel of Mercy."

He snorted at that last example.

"And you ... you were the Witness. But witnesses are inherently passive, never taking the lead role. Despite that, here you are, taking a decidedly proactive role. You know, bringing about the apocalypse and all."

He nodded. For the first time, I saw genuine excitement paint his face. "Yes, that is exactly correct."

"You need me to be the witness. To all that you are about to do."

"Yes. Very good, Katrina. Very good, indeed."

"The only question I have is ... why me?"

↔

A silence hung between us as my question sat unanswered. "No lies, remember?" I repeated.

Still, he said nothing.

"And omissions are a form of—"

"Lying, yes. I know. But whereas I truly desire to tell you, I do not know if you are ready to hear the truth."

"The truth being ..."

"That this was your destiny, woven into the fabric of time so long ago."

"OK, let's add being cryptic as a form of lying. Oh, and deduct you major points for being creepy, too."

Enoch chuckled. "Yes, I suppose you are right. Let me give you *part* of the truth now. A nibble, if you will, to satiate your curiosity. I learned that the gods would leave even before the gods themselves had formulated their little plans."

"How?" Curiosity overwhelmed me. Hell, it overwhelmed everyone. Even Egya looked up, giving him that head tilt dogs do when you have their full attention. This guy should have written a book. And that wasn't sarcasm. He really should have … It would be a massive bestseller that would most likely outsell the Bible, Koran and Torah combined.

"Long before you were born, I was a witness to the three Sisters of Fate, and they showed me the thread that led to this point." He stared off into the distance, lost in his own memories. "It was the only time I used my position to gain knowledge that should not have been mine.

"They showed me the gods departure, my unfortunate humanity and you, my dear Katrina. And they told me that our destinies are intertwined. That you would bring me before the gods for one final judgment.

"But the Fates, being the Fates, did not tell all. I do not know what that final judgement will be, nor do I know when. But that is why I chose you. Why I have followed you for all this time."

I stood there, flabbergasted. This guy had literally been stalking me since I was born. Hell, since *before* I was born.

As cosmically weirded out as I was, I needed to keep my cool if I was going to get out of this. I had one more move to make. It was a long shot, but when you're screwed, sometimes long shots are all you get.

"What about our pending nuptials? Did they tell you about that, too?"

Enoch paused as his face betrayed a momentary panic. But as quickly as that panic showed itself, it disappeared, his demeanor returning to its normal calm, confident, smug self.

Still, it was there. I'd touched a nerve.

"My dear, no, they did not show us together in any other capacity than our intertwined fates. Still, I know. I know because I have—"

"Because you have what? Used one of those eye thingies to see the future? I know that's not true. If it were, you would never have let this little scene unfold, would you?" I paused, searching for the truth in my words. Given his reaction—or rather, his lack of a reaction—I knew I had guessed right. He hadn't seen the future. He only spoke of the future he hoped for. Which meant that he didn't actually know if he'd ever see the gods again. This was all open.

I narrowed my eyes as if I was struggling to understand what was happening here. "You are so damn confident that we're going to wind up together. How? Why? I mean, we've never met. Sure, you've been pinning the celestial versions of pervy photos on your cosmic walls, but that doesn't mean—"

"Because I know you," Enoch rasped. "I know you better than you know yourself."

"How cliché. Did you read that in *Villains for Dummies,* or was that particular gem something you picked up in Villainy 101?" I threw in as much ire and contempt as I could, summoning every ounce of the intonation partners have used on their lovers since the dawn of time. The tone that clearly says, *"I'm not impressed."*

As I used it, images of all my past boyfriends throwing up their arms in exasperation flew through my mind. All two of them: Justin and Aldie—the dark elf I dated about a hundred and fifty years ago.

Boy oh boy, I really am inexperienced on the boyfriend front.

Lovers and victims, on the other hand …

Enoch, much like those two, threw up his arms and head before returning his gaze to me in that way that said, *"We're about to get into it now, girl."*

Good. Finally my feminine wiles were working.

Enoch began to utter something when I lifted a hand. "Ah-ah-ah. Before you hit me with whatever priceless gem you have swimming in that head of yours, answer me this, *Megatron …*"

That did it. He flew into a rage in that way I just knew he would.

36

You don't stalk someone for centuries without being a wee bit unbalanced. The trick is to find the axis ... and kick it.

"*Metatron*," he growled, and I don't know if it was real or not, but I felt Deirdre's grip on me lighten. It wasn't much, but it was definitely there.

I don't know much about magic. As a vampire, we never had the ability to burn time. All our magic tended to be inherent abilities that were "on" all the time. But I did date that fae guy, and he told me that spells generally fall into one of two camps: timed or concentration.

Timed spells are just that ... magical effects that, once they run their course, are over. A fireball is done and gone once it hits its target. A summoned demon only hangs around for as long as the spell is designed to last. Once that timer buzzes, the creature either goes back to wherever it came from, or is free to do whatever it wants (which usually results in attacking the summoner. Funny thing about summoning demons: they don't like being pulled away from their fire-and-brimstone homes).

But concentration spells are different. They require the caster to be focused on the spell's effects. The more powerful the caster, the more spells they can cast simultaneously.

That takes experience and intelligence—something Enoch had in abundance, given how many spells he had going at once while dealing with me.

But no matter how much experience and intelligence you might have, someone like little ol' *moi* will find a way to make you falter, and that was exactly what was happening now.

All that was left was to push him just that little bit more.

"Let me guess," I said, "they never said anything about us getting married, but after centuries of watching me, you fell in love and convinced yourself that I'd do the same once I got to know you. So this little rendezvous ... is it going as planned? Are my knees wobbling? Am I swooning? Tell me, archangel formerly known as Metatron, am I falling in love with you?"

I hit the *you* hard, lacing it with as much venomous hatred as I could. Which wasn't hard, given that I really did hate this guy.

Enoch threw his arms up in the air, twirling on his heels in a way that made me think he was going to storm off. Wouldn't that have been nice? But a guy like him doesn't walk away from a fight. They turn to confront whomever is pissing them.

And that is exactly what he did. Good thing I was ready for him.

7

FRIENDS DON'T LET FRIENDS TIME TRAVEL

*H*e turned around to look his aggravator in her beautiful, sky-blue eyes, but instead of being met by a shade of blue that makes you dream of rainbows (hey, I have amazing eyes, no sense in being humble about it), he was greeted by the same contact lens he'd used on me earlier.

What's more, I forced both Egya and Deirdre to look me in the eyes, too, stimulating their greatest desires.

And currently, that desire was to be free of this asshole.

I held Enoch's gaze as I said, "You two, get out of here." I noted that Egya hadn't transformed back. He was still in hyena form, which was both a good and bad thing.

Good because, as a hyena, he could bite. Something he did right away, snapping the Eye of Borvo out of Enoch's hand. Bad because, as much as his constant cackling annoyed me, I could have really used some sort of witty quip right about now.

"Go," I said, "before he does something else to you two." I beckoned Deirdre over.

She took a few steps toward me. "But milady, I must stay by your side and—"

I pulled the pendant from around my neck and pressed it into her hand. "Deirdre, for the love of the GoneGods, just go."

I heard Egya growl, and the pulling and ripping of fabric as he tugged at Deirdre. That was followed by reluctant footsteps and the slamming of a car door. They were in Egya's car, driving away. But given that Egya had paws, I guessed Deirdre was the driver. She could barely ride the bus without incident, and I lamented any driver who got the full brunt of her road rage.

They were gone, which left Enoch and me alone. The Soul Jar was gone. Given all that, I was free to do what needed to be done.

I wasn't entirely sure how the contact lens worked. It stimulated one's desires, but I'd eventually broken out of its spell, which meant that he would, too.

Walking over to him, I unbuttoned the top two buttons of my blouse. I figured I'd fan the flames of his desire, and in a voice that was as sincere as my acting abilities allowed, I said, "You were right. We do belong together. We are one and the same, fates intertwined. Two souls, one destiny." Yuck. But hey, these were exactly the kinds of words that got an angel going: fate, love, destiny.

Making love to an angel was the stuff of NC-17, steamy romance novels.

I took a step forward, reaching my hand out to him. He returned the gesture, his eyes misty with the anticipation of love finally requited.

Another step and I'd be next to him. *He's just a man,* I kept saying to myself. *He's just a man. And men have snappable necks.* I just needed to get close enough to—

But as soon as our fingers touched, I didn't just feel his skin. I felt *him.* All of him. The world started to whirl as the two of us were transported to another realm.

No, not another realm … another time.

We were in the distant past. A time Enoch called "home."

"Crap," I mumbled as I stared around the sparse wooden shack. "More magic."

PART II

INTERMISSION:

"Giants walk this Earth," the wounded angel says, "but they should not."

Enoch, the mortal human, is young, virile and strong. He is also crouched beside the largest angel he's ever seen: Oche.

The massive angel grabs at his side, his hand over an open wound where light—an angel's blood—pours out of him.

Enoch is a healer, but only for humans. He has no idea how to heal an angel.

Oche grunts in pain. "God did not wish for such creatures to be born. He did not ordain their existence. I am sure of it. But my brethren—" His words are cut off by a sudden and violent cough; spittles of light drip from his lips.

"You have internal bleeding," Enoch says as he prepares his tourniquet. "I must close the wound for you to have any hope of surviving."

Enoch pulls out the largest needle in his kit, a needle he fashioned from the bones of a whale that washed up on the shores near his village. He made it more as a pretty trinket than with any intent to use. Even though it is the size of his middle finger and as sharp as anything he's ever made, he doubts it will be enough.

"Hold still," Enoch says.

Oche tries to move. "I must return to the battle. Help my fellow warriors. I am a soldier in God's army. I am—"

"A creature who is about to die. Do you understand me? You will die if you insist on moving."

Oche returns Enoch's gaze as if confused.

Enoch, for all the limitations of his mortality, understands. "Tell me, angel. What will happen to you should you die?"

Oche says nothing.

"Do you have a soul like humans do? Something that will usher you to the afterlife?"

Again, his question is met with silence.

"Is there even an afterlife for angels?"

Oche starts to speak, but quickly falls silent.

"From your silence, I gather that the answer is no, or perhaps you do not know. Either way, I suspect it is best you let me help you than gamble on your very existence."

What Enoch does not add is that the mere act of this surgery is a gamble. He doubts the angel will live through the procedure, let alone the night.

Oche stares deep into Enoch's eyes before nodding. "Very well." The giant creature lays back down on the ground, and Enoch begins his arduous task of saving an angel's life.

↔

The angel sits surprisingly still during the surgery. No easy feat, given Enoch has no herbs to dull the pain, no remedies to send this creature to sleep. The creature does wince and groan, but other than those minor expressions of pain, he doesn't move a feather.

Once Enoch is done, he turns to Oche. "Does your kind sleep?"

"On occasion."

"Then sleep."

Oche does not close his eyes.

"Please," Enoch begs. "You need to heal, and your body requires rest."

Oche looks at the shack's door.

"The war will still be here tomorrow," Enoch says. "And you will be all the more capable of fighting then."

In truth, Enoch doubts the angel will be here tomorrow. It is a miracle that he is still here now.

Eventually Oche nods, closing his eyes. Whether it is the exhaustion of battle or the toll of his wounds, the angel drifts to sleep almost as soon as his eyes close, leaving Enoch to clean his other wounds.

Deep slashes pierce the angel's incredibly tough hide, bruises the size of boulders spotting his body.

"What kind of creature could inflict so much damage on one such as you, Oche?" Enoch murmurs.

↔

The next morning comes, and Oche's eyes open with the light of dawn. The angel sits up, his head brushing against the roof of Enoch's shack.

Enoch cannot hide his surprise. "I did not think this day would smile upon you."

Oche winces, touching the wound on his side. Whereas yesterday it was deep, today it looks little more than a scratch.

"God in Heaven." Enoch's head goes dizzy. "You are almost healed. How?"

"I am a soldier in God's army. We are not so easily killed."

"Still, whatever being that hurt you—"

"A giant," Oche spits out. "A creature I have never seen before. But as we fought, I saw the holy symbol of Azazel on its neck."

43

Oche speaks as if that explains all, but Enoch does not understand.

Oche grows impatient with Enoch's ignorance of the ways of angels. "Only those sired by us can share our name. This creature, this unholy creation, must be Azazel's child." Oche shakes his head. "But it is forbidden for an angel to fornicate with a human. If my assertion is right, then Azazel has broken a holy law."

"Such a union is possible?"

Oche nods. "It should not be, as it is forbidden, but many of my brethren chose to defy God's will."

"How? Why?" Enoch says. "God's words are final. Who would dare defy Him?"

"I do not understand it myself. But what I do know with all my being is that war is coming between those loyal to God and those who chose human pleasures of eternal glory. War. And if more of those monsters should walk the Earth, I do not know if the side of light can prevail."

↔

Oche stays with Enoch one more day and night, waiting until his wounds heal.

Once the angel is fully rested, he leaves Enoch's hut. "Where will you go now?"

Oche points to the east. "Beyond that mountain is where the battle took place. I will go there, see what came of it and report back to the heavens above."

"And should you encounter that creature again?"

"I will fight it."

"Alone? You barely survived fighting it before. I suggest that your purpose be not to die this day, but to warn others."

Oche contemplates the mortal's words. The human is right. Still, to walk away from battle, a challenge ... that goes against Oche's very nature.

Unfurling his wings, Oche prepares to take to the sky. But in the moment before he leaves, he hears the mortal utter, "Take me with you."

The mortal's hands are clenched in fists as his body shakes with obvious fear. But there is also resolve in his eyes. "Take me with you. Should other angels be wounded, they will need me."

Enoch does not wait for Oche's response, running into his hut to gather his supplies. "Take me with you," the brave human repeats. "Take me so that I may serve."

↔

They return to the site of the battle. There are many wounded. Many dead. Enoch walks among the dead angels and remarks how their bodies look like the same empty shells, just like any human body. They even bleed. Granted, their blood is made of light, but still it stains their body.

But there is one difference: the expression on their faces. It is that of deep sadness. True despair.

Later, he will understand that death for an angel is final. There is no second life. There is no Heaven.

There is nothing.

Oche walks among the dead, tears of light streaming down his face. "I should have been here," the angel says.

Enoch shakes his head. "With your wounds, you would have only perished with them. At least now you can avenge your fallen brethren."

Oche pounds his chest with his left hand. "This I swear."

A groan sounds. There among the dead is one angel. She sits upright, her back against a rock, her hand still on her sword. Oche immediately goes to her side. "Miral. Captain—you live."

Miral looks up, and in her pain and delirium she struggles to focus on Oche. But as the two rush closer, she realizes that this is not a dream. One of her fellow angels has survived.

"How? How …" she manages. "I saw you fall from the sky."

"I did. I would have perished had it not been for this human who found me. He saved me."

Miral looks at the human, Enoch. "And your reward shall be the Kingdom of Heaven."

"I need no reward," Enoch says.

At this, Miral chuckles. "Need and deserve are often at odds." Then, reaching a hand for Oche, "Help me up. Perhaps together we can—"

But before she can finish her thought, a great howl pierces the field. Enoch turns to see seven giants rushing from the forest, brandishing clubs made from broken tree trunks.

Behind them stands one unassuming boy. He looks like an ordinary human child, except his eyes are lit with an ancient wisdom beyond that of any mere mortal.

The child lets out a vicious cry of war as he points at Enoch and the angels. Immediately and without hesitation, the giants charge at them.

Oche picks up Miral's sword. "Fools." Then, faster than thought, he moves through them, slicing all seven giants with the Blade of God. All fall. "They blindly obey their master, even if it means death."

"They are compelled to obey him." Miral tries to stand. Her leg is severely broken, as is her left wing. She cannot walk. She cannot fly. She is helpless.

Oche turns the blade on the child who shows no fear. "You are next, child."

"No," Miral says. "You stand no chance. Run, Oche. Run."

"Never."

"I order you."

"Then I disobey." Oche has resigned himself to die this day. He is also determined to make it glorious.

But before he can foolishly attack the boy, a soft hand touches him. The human Enoch is standing by his side. "Give me the sword."

"What?"

"Let me fight this abomination. Should I fall—*when* I fall," Enoch corrects himself, "I will meet you in Heaven."

Oche looks down, astonished by this human's bravery.

"Please, help your fallen friend. I will distract the boy."

Oche hesitates before nodding. There is much wisdom in the human's words. Much wisdom, and even greater sacrifice.

He hands Enoch the sword and goes to Miral. Cradling her like a father would his child, he only takes a moment to say, "Thank you, Enoch. Your sacrifice will be forever remembered."

And with that, Oche takes to the sky, leaving the human Enoch to face off against a creature that killed a legion of angels.

↔

Enoch has never held a sword before, but it seems simple enough. Stab the enemy with the pointy end.

He charges at the boy, who does not move. The child just waits for Enoch to get close and as the mortal swings the Blade of God at him, the child simply lifts one hand.

The sword—the Blade of God—is instantly transformed into a thousand butterflies that float away in the wind.

"What? How?" Enoch says.

The child's eyes hollow out as he summons his magic. Then, putting a hand on the crown of Enoch's head, Enoch feels a sharp pain as his mind is dug into. "Why do you fight for them?" the child asks.

"I fight for the righteous. I fight for God."

"You know not what you fight for," the child says. "You simply follow an old script handed to you."

"And what do you fight for?" Enoch falls to his knees. His head feels as though it will shatter like a clay pot.

"I fight for everything," the child says. And with those words, he squeezes. Enoch knows that he is about to die.

He knows that soon he will be with his God.

But just as the sweet release of death is about to take him, the child stops. His eyes cease their maniacal glow, returning to their normal state. He looks at Enoch with confusion as a single, human tear that is not made of light rolls down his cheek.

"You are my brother's keeper," the child says. True bewilderment envelops the child as he speaks.

"I know not your brother," Enoch responds.

The child stares at Enoch, his expression a mixture of love and fear. "You are his keeper. You are his—"

The boy's words are interrupted by a blade thrusting out of his chest, and Enoch sees an angel of great stature standing behind him.

Lifting the skewered boy up, Enoch sees the child trying to summon more magic. But before he can, the angel uses his massive hand to crush his skull.

The child is dead.

"What did the Nephilim say to you?"

Enoch is so confused. What happened? Where did this angel come from? "Nothing. Nothing I ... I understood."

The angel nods. "More tricks. More lies, I am sure." Then he smiles at Enoch. "Thank you, human, for distracting the creature. You allowed me to get close enough to end him. I am the archangel Michael, and I understand that it is because of you that both Miral and Oche live. You have done well. Come, there is someone who wishes to meet you."

Michael outstretches his blood-soaked hand. Enoch hesitates before taking it in his.

As soon as he does, Michael takes to the sky, lifting Enoch with him as they ascend to Heaven.

End to Part 2

8

WHAT A ROMANTIC GETAWAY

"So that's how you got your wings," I said.

Enoch nodded. "I always admired your ability to quip during moments of intense emotion. It is both your greatest quality and your most grating quirk."

"That's me, a bundle of 'what are we going to do with her?' " But the truth was, even I was surprised that I could joke at a moment like this. Not only had I seen Enoch's creation—I'd felt it, too. As sure as I would have if I had been Enoch himself, I'd felt it.

And not only that moment, but all his moments. I knew everything this man had ever experienced. Not only experienced, but also felt, endured, thought … everything.

I was trying my best to not let the magnitude of that experience weaken me. Truth was, I didn't know if I could. It was rare to experience something so intimate and then go right back to hero-nemesis banter.

Still, a girl's gotta try.

"Looks like my stalker just got stalked," I mused.

Enoch ignored me, still nostalgic. "Yes, that is exactly how I got my wings, as you put it. A living human cannot exist in Heaven for long. The mere magnitude of such a place weighs heavily, and the human mind … well, the human mind is not designed to be able to hold such things. So my reward for saving Oche was eternal life … up to a point. But I have long contemplated the events of that day and the days that came after. I suspect I was not being rewarded for saving the angel, but rather talking sense into him. Sense that ultimately led to the second of the two angel wars."

"The second?"

Enoch nodded. "The second war was for lust. The first was for pride, but that is another story." Sighing, he closed his eyes as a single tear found its way down his cheek. "Now that you know me thus, do you see why I believe our union is inevitable? To know someone—to truly see their soul—is to love them. We are bound, you and me. Now and forever."

He was right … I wanted to hate Enoch. I truly did. Had I not just seen everything—and I mean *everything*—about the man who became an archangel, I might have been able to. But when you knew someone, hatred just isn't possible.

Enoch was right: we were bound, and as much as I didn't want to admit it, I could see that bond growing into something more.

I shuddered at the thought and, if I was being truly honest with myself, that shudder wasn't just because the thoughts of being with a man like him were bad. I also shuddered at how good it would be, too.

Enoch was crying, kneeling before me. I only needed to reach out and snap his neck and it would be done. I really wanted to, after all. Ending this here and now was the best thing for me, my friends, not to mention the Earth and everyone on it.

I'd seen enough in my three hundred years to know that an obsessed maniac like this guy wasn't going to stop. Not ever. And as much as we idealize many of the Marvel superheroes who never cross the line by actually killing their nemeses, they're naïve.

In the game of monsters, solutions need to be final.

And here we were, two of the worst monsters I knew, face to face.

As much as I wanted to take advantage of his weakened state, I just couldn't. I had seen too much. I understood too much. This man—for that is what he was, a human man—had seen and endured so much. It's amazing he wasn't a blubbering mess of flesh and drool.

"You have to stop," I whispered. "Find a way to embrace your mortality. Find a way to be human."

Enoch's tears continued to pour down his face as he nodded—as in, he was agreeing with me.

"You … you knew that would happen, didn't you?" I said. "You knew that touching you would result in … in whatever that was."

"Aye." The word came out as a whispered rasp. "I did. It is one of the perks of being a creature of Heaven. A *former* creature of Heaven," he corrected. "Up there, when two souls meet, connect, they learn all there is about each other. So that the relationship, be it a simple friendship or more, starts from a moment of pure understanding. It was the only way that human souls could truly connect in harmony. Our souls have touched, Katrina—they have gone through the transformation. Just because we were not there to experience it directly does not negate what our souls already know. I knew that when we touched, you would see all there was to see about what I am. Who I am."

Enoch closed his eyes, swept away by the sanctity of the moment. "Love is patient, love is kind. It does not envy, it does not boast, it is not proud," he rasped. "It does not dishonor others, it is not self-seeking, it is not easily angered, it keeps no record of wrongs. Love does not delight in evil, but rejoices in the truth. It always protects, always trusts, always hopes, always perseveres. Love never fails. But where there are prophecies, they will cease; where there are tongues, they will be stilled; where there is knowledge, it will pass away."

"1 Corinthians 13," I said. "It was my father's favorite passage."

"I know. In that, if nothing else, your father and I are alike. But do you know what it means? Truly means?"

I rolled my eyes. "Let me guess, you're about to mansplain it to me?"

If Enoch got the reference, he ignored me. "Love is often spoken about in the Bible. Most humans interpret it in the manner that their limited capacity allows. *True* love is the ability to know each other, just as we two do now. And once we have that knowledge, hate can never fill our hearts."

I could see it, too. In a divisive world of nations, ethnicities and religions—hell, of Democrats and Republicans—the only way they could all get along up there and still retain a bit of who they were on Earth was to truly understand each other. That understanding would remove the strangeness between them. And once that was gone, so too would fear and hatred disappear, leaving behind only love.

"Brilliant," I muttered.

Enoch chuckled. "It was my suggestion when I became Metatron. It was how we ensured humans could live in harmony, up there in Heaven. And it was the only piece of consultation that He thanked me for directly." He spoke with a kind of humbled pride. "Being thanked by Him was the greatest achievement of my life."

I wiped away an escaped tear. "And you?" I asked. "Have you seen me? Everything I've done over my own life? All the murders, killing, feedings?"

He shook his head. "My soul has yet to be returned to me."

"That's what I thought. Because if you had seen what a truly terrible monster I was, you wouldn't—"

"No, you are wrong." Enoch got to his feet. "I have seen who you are. Since before you were born, I have watched you and everything you have done."

"But you haven't felt it."

"I do not need to." He took my hand in his.

Thank the GoneGods that touching again didn't send us on another trip down memory lane.

↔

We both looked at each other for a long, awkward moment before the silence was finally broken by a simple statement rasped by a man who would never abandon his mission. *"Now do you see why I want my soul oh so desperately?"*

"Oh yeah, that's what got us into this mess." I chuckled.

"Indeed." He nodded.

"Yay," I said. "Good to see that I'm still me, quirks and all."

"My soul," he repeated, putting out his other hand. "Please." His eyes held a quiet desperation.

So, in his mesmerized state he had deeply wanted us to touch so we could *know* each other. But now that that was done, his motivations had shifted. And because I still wore the contact lens, they were being stirred.

He was showing his truest desire.

I nodded. "OK, but first: will you abandon your plans to destroy this world?"

He shook his head with a vehement honesty I hadn't expected.

"Why not? Surely there are other ways to follow the gods that don't require everyone to die. I've seen who you are—what you know. If anyone can find a path, it's you."

"Perhaps, but such a path will take centuries. Human technology needs to advance considerably. Research will take decades of effort. Sadly, this mortal coil will not provide us with the time needed."

"So they all have to die." I gestured to the people around us with my free hand.

"They all have to be freed from a life of pain and suffering," Enoch said.

I let out a deep breath as I closed my eyes, a tear releasing from within me. "That's what all fanatics say. 'The infidels must die, but we do not see that as murder, for really, we are freeing them.' Such final words from the very ones who need to be freed from this life."

Enoch's arm stiffened as he saw where this conversation was going.

So I did the only thing I could.

I punched him. Square in the nose.

↔

My punch sent him flying back. And although my attack was meant to hurt him, it was also meant to free me. That's the thing about surprise hits right in the kisser: both hands tend to let go of whatever they're holding and fly straight up to the face to protect against the next blow.

Enoch took several steps back; my blow wasn't strong enough to knock him on his ass. As he staggered, I stepped back until I felt the edge of the sidewalk. One more step and I'd be on the road. Good.

As soon as Enoch got a hold of himself, he gave me a look that reminded me of hurt puppies. As in, multiple puppies. (The guy was really good at looking pitiable.) But there was also confusion mixed in there, like he didn't really understand why I'd done that.

That's the trouble with fanatics: they never understand why someone else just doesn't see it their way.

"I'm not going to let you end the world just so you can get more kudos from the Big Guy. Sorry."

"You fool." His eyes narrowed. "Perhaps I misunderstood you. Perhaps I saw in you something that never was there."

"If you're referring to a mass murderer who's OK with genocide, yeah, I think you probably were projecting there."

Enoch fumbled for something in his pocket, which meant that he had another magical item in his pocket. Not good.

And given that I had no idea what it did, I wasn't sure if I should run, divert my gaze, or start singing really loudly so I couldn't hear any incantations.

He pulled out an earring of all things, and taking the hook end of it, put it in his ear.

Thing was, his ears weren't pierced, so he really needed to dig the thing in. Something he did with brutal efficiency and way faster than I could put my own earrings in … and I had several piercings (and not only in my ears, ahem).

"I offered you the world, Katrina," he said. "More than the world. I offered you universes, life eternal, and you rejected it. And for what? Stupid talking monkeys."

"Yeah. What are you going to do?"

I really wished I hadn't asked that question.

He lifted both his hands and spoke in the manner that I imagined an Aztec priest did just before plunging an obsidian blade in the sacrificial belly of some poor soul. "Come to me. Now."

In the airport, though the glass windows and sliding doors, I saw dozens of people and Others stop what they were doing. Conversations, hugging, walking—they all just stopped and turned their heads in our direction.

Then they began filing outside.

Within a minute there must have been over fifty people standing behind him, many of them still dragging their luggage behind.

The zombie army of would-be travelers stared at me with hollow eyes, and all I could think about was how these guys would all miss their flights because this asshole had cast a spell on them. I also wondered if travel insurance now covered enchantments and other acts of Other-related activity.

In this new GoneGod World, it should. It really should.

Enoch smirked. "One last chance."

I considered it. I really did. I thought about how easy it would be to give in, return his soul to him and, hell, to go on the ultimate road trip. But then an image of my father flashed through my mind. What would he do? The right thing, of course. Without hesitation.

That was who I wanted to be.

"Thanks Dad," I murmured as the wicked smile of resolve crept along my face.

Enoch tilted his head in confusion, and I de-confused him by giving him my final answer in the form of my middle finger.

Way to be mature, Kat.

9

MOB MENTALITY AND MAGICAL SYNERGY

*H*ave you ever fought an angry mob? Sadly, I have. And I can say with full confidence that it sucks. Royally.

Well, that's not entirely true. When I was a soulless creature of the night, fighting a mob was the only time I could really let loose. The beast of the vampire would come out in a no-holds-barred, Hulk-Hogan-meets-Wolverine kind of way.

It was the only time I truly connected with the real demon within. The berserker who only cared for the kill. Allowing so much power to be unleased, testing the full potential of my vampiric body and knowing that the battle could only end in death—either theirs or mine—was intoxicating.

But fighting a spellbound mob of innocents as a human? Not so much.

For one thing, I had to hold back, doing my best not to inflict any permanent damage on any of these guys.

For another, getting punched in this human body hurt.

"Ow!" I screamed as a manananggal demon swung her carry-on at me. From the thud her bag made, I took it she had one of those old-school laptops in there. *Ever heard of a MacBook Air, lady?*

I managed to duck under the wild swing of a human yacha bozu as a chain-filled leather jacket rattled overhead. The only boon to fighting this crowd was that none of them were warriors.

Well, maybe the demon with her indestructible laptop.

A security guard pulled out his baton and charged. Waiting for him to get close enough, I dropped to my knees and punched him square in his ... well, you know. He crumbled, dropping his baton like a cat presenting a dead bird. But even keeled over, he still reached for me, the spell in direct conflict with his natural reaction to pain.

Can't we give this poor guy a break? I thought as I easily swatted his hand away.

Picking up the baton, I knocked two nixes in their chins. Stepping on the back of the still-keeled-over security guard, I launched into the air, kicking another human in the face while knocking a kijimuna on his laurel-crowned head with the baton.

Then five more charged at me, and in the flurry of twists, punches and kicks, I couldn't even see what they were.

Most people think fighting multiple opponents is harder than just taking on one at a time. That might be true *if* the multiple opponents knew what they were doing and coordinated their attacks. Such an onslaught would quickly tire you and eventually you'd drop from exhaustion, making you easy pickings.

But when the mob wasn't trained and didn't know how to work together ... well, that was a whole different kind of battle. The two best ways to beat *that* kind of attack were to use their uncoordinated attacks against each other ... and to not hold back.

I'd let loose as a vampire in the past, and I'd have to let loose as human now. Summoning all my training in aikido, judo and Krav Maga, I let it all out, going for the most effective moves to put my attackers out of commission. So much for not doing any permanent damage. I'd like to say that I felt guilt over hurting these innocents. But my bigger 'yes' at this moment was surviving, and the truth was, the feral part of me enjoyed pushing this body to its limits.

I poked the human on my left with a finger to his eye, and using the momentum of a Chinese tulou, I guided the horned creature to batter the Korean Dokkaebi in the chest. That was four of them down, leaving only the mul guishin standing.

The terrifying, ghost-like girl just stood there, not attacking. But from the way her hand went up before going down again, I could sense an inner conflict. She didn't want to fight me, but was still being compelled to do so.

Seeing me defeat the others must have allowed some kind of survival instinct to kick in … a survival instinct that countered Enoch's spell.

Which meant his magic had limits.

I assessed my options. So far, only eight members of the mob had attacked me. The rest held back, as if in reserve. But then again, maybe not. Enoch might have been holding back … or there were serious limits to his power.

After all, he wasn't burning time—he was using magical items imbued with power. Perhaps there *were* limits. Like, he could only send a couple charmed travelers at me at one time. Or maybe he was conserving his charges. I'd heard of some items only being able to produce a handful of fireballs before becoming perfectly ordinary trinkets again. Maybe this magic worked the same way.

I knew that the smart thing was to get out of here. Run away. But if his magic could be drained, then that was my best bet for defeating him. So looking Enoch straight in the eyes, I said, "Even *you* have limits."

Standing, I turned my gaze on the ambling crowd and cried out in my best Brad-Pitt-as-Achilles voice, "Is there no one else?" (A great scene in an otherwise meh movie, and part of me brimmed with pride that I could use the iconic line here.)

Enoch laughed. But given his total lack of interest in human culture, I doubted he'd seen the movie. Which meant he was amused by something else. He wagged an admonishing finger at me. "Very clever."

I gave him a curtsey.

"Yes, you are right. Many of the magics I can employ do have limits and must be used in tandem to get the desired results. For example, I summoned this crowd with the lump of dough."

"Dough? Seriously, how is uncooked bread magical?"

"It belonged to Moses and—"

"These travelers are your Israelites?" I was going to have to be a Biblical scholar to defeat this guy.

"Very good. And yes, that is exactly what the dough does. Summons travelers, and since we are in an airport ..."

"You decided to use it to hijack them."

"But the dough can only summon." He dropped it on the ground. "And only once." As soon as the impossibly-old-and-yet-not-moldy dough hit the ground, he stepped on it. The travelers behind him started to sway, as if anxious to move.

"Then I used this little item to charm them to do my bidding." He took off one of his rings.

"Let me guess ... it's the one ring to bind them all."

He tilted his head. "Indeed. How would you know such a thing?" From his intonation, I gathered he had never read Tolkien, but that Tolkien had read and been inspired by whatever grimoire or ancient tome had that item in it.

Enoch rotated the ring between his fingers. "Silvinus's Ring is said to curse those nearby into doing its wearer's bidding. But only for a time. And the more dangerous the request, the less likely they are to do my bidding."

He pocketed the ring. I guessed it could be used more than once. "Your prowess in battle has made these people less inclined to attack you. To that end, I must say I am impressed. Few could dispatch so many at once. You are a formidable warrior."

I cracked my neck from side to side before dropping into my best kung fu pose. Then flipping over my extended hand, I gestured for Enoch to approach. "A warrior who's going to kick your ass all the way to Tuesday."

Did I just say that? Oh well. The only way to embrace a tired cliché is to make it true.

I charged at Enoch.

10

'YOU HAVEN'T SEEN THE LAST OF ME' IS SOMETHING VILLAINS SAY

I've been in a lot of fights. Despite the last few months of my life, most of them have taken place in some dojo against a martial arts master. I've learned how to deal with opponents who were bigger, stronger and faster than me. I've practiced countless moves and counter-moves, all designed to help me win.

Or, at the very least, to help me not make a fool out of myself.

So when I charged Enoch, I expected him to get into some defensive stance or try to hit me before I could hit him.

What I didn't expect was for him to do nothing. And in my arrogance, I thought that he had frozen, terrified of little ol' *moi*.

Perhaps he couldn't believe the love of his life was going to kick his ass. Or perhaps he just couldn't believe I would dare attack him. After all, gods used to kneel before him.

Seeing my advantage, I upgraded what was intended to be a conservative move to—and I quote *The Incredible Hulk* here—SMASH.

I leapt into the air, seeking to drive my fist down hard onto the bridge of his nose. Not only would this break his nose, it would blind him, too. And if I put enough force behind the strike, it could knock him out.

Even with me in midair, he still didn't move. He didn't even look up to watch me come down on him. My fist connected, but instead of hearing the oh-so-satisfying crunch of cracking cartilage and bone, there was a dull thud as my fist exploded in pain.

I had broken at least two fingers on his face. Badly.

"Ahh." I cradled my right hand. "What the f—?"

He sighed, showing me what looked like a small tin can of Vaseline. "A salve made from the rock bed of the River Styx. After your little move in the airport security room, I decided to use the same water Thetis did to make her child, Achilles, invulnerable."

"Another gift?" I was trying to buy myself some time while setting my two broken fingers straight. I would need this hand if I was going to keep fighting, so bracing myself, I pulled at them, resetting the bones with a horrific crack.

I grimaced in pain, but I didn't cry. Not even a little bit … Those tears were because I got some dust in my eyes. Honest.

Enoch shook his head. "Actually, this was something I made for myself. There was a brief period in my immortal life when I thought I should have taken a more active role in human development. I arrogantly believed that I could convince the gods to stay by forcing humankind to become more pious."

"Tomás De Torquemada shit again?"

"Indeed. That was the original design for the Inquisition—to remind humanity of God's will through—"

"Torture and death."

"Through sacrifice and resolve. Unfortunately, humans tend to hear the message and then take it one step too far. That was an unfortunate time, and one that did not influence the gods into reconsidering their abandonment."

"No kidding." As we spoke, I was trying to find some kind of leverage to fight this guy. I could attack him, but not with the salve on him. Maybe I could give him a bath first? Given that he wanted to marry me, he'd probably be into that.

Who was I kidding? There was no way out of this now. I needed to escape. Run. Regroup and figure shit out.

I needed to get the Soul Jar to the archangel Michael in Paradise Lot and wash my hands of the problem.

If anyone could beat a former archangel, it would be an actual archangel, right?

"What now?" I thought. Well, I thought I'd thought it.

"Now?" A sad smile adorned Enoch's otherwise stoic face. "Now this ends. For you, at least."

↔

In a blur of speed and grace, he grabbed me, lifting me overhead as one hand pushed against me and the other wrapped around my neck. He was impossibly strong. I mean, I've fought actual superheroes (long story) with super strength, and I could still get their arms to budge a little bit. But striking down on his elbow was like hitting an iron pole. It didn't bend in the least.

"When I tried to kill myself up in Heaven, one technique I employed was strangulation. Hence the scars on my neck. What I forgot was how long it takes for a human to die from lack of breath." He squeezed a little more. "And how painful it is."

As he held me above him, my feet dangling several inches above the ground, an old lady walked under the arc of his arm like we weren't even there. So much for a Good Samaritan coming to my rescue.

"Wait," I tried to mumble, but under the pressure of his hand I couldn't say anything.

A minivan pulled up, letting out several kids dressed in baseball uniforms. Two overly enthusiastic kids bumped into Enoch, momentarily looking up at him before shrugging and running inside.

So people might not notice him, but they could bump into him. And that nudge did cause Enoch to loosen his grip enough for me to take one breath.

As soon as the kids were inside and the minivan was gone, Enoch resumed crushing my larynx as he took a few steps toward the road to avoid being interrupted by any other passengers rushing into the airport.

"You broke my heart, Katrina. I truly believed that we would be together, but seeing your insolence, I know that to be false now. I will have to continue without you. I shall have to hunt down the were-hyena and changeling to retrieve my soul."

Damn it, so he'd seen my little sleight-of-hand trick.

"But because I do still possess genuine affection for you, I promise you this: their deaths will be swift and painless. In fact, I will go one step further. They won't even know what hit—"

Just as he was about to finish his sentence, a friggin' bus rolled up onto the sidewalk and crashed right into him.

↔

The driver managed to get far enough onto the curb to avoid hitting me, too, catching Enoch all the way to the elbow. The momentum of the blow caused him to fly forward, dropping me in the process.

Before I could even get my bearings, powerful hands picked me up and guided me to the open bus door, where—

"You've got to be friggin' kidding me. You couldn't drive?" I said, turning to Deirdre.

"I have never attempted to operate an automobile," the changeling said as she pulled the lever, closing the bus door.

"You still would have been a better choice than him," I said.

Egya's hyena form chortled as the canine sat in the driver's seat. Two front paws were dutifully positioned at the 4- and 8-o'clock positions on the steering wheel. His hind legs were on the accelerator and brake as his body sat at what looked like a terribly uncomfortable angle—for a dog, at least.

At least when Enoch turned him, Egya was big enough to reach it all and still be able to see over the dashboard … Thank the GoneGods for small—or rather, big enough—miracles.

"Move over," I said, looking out the front window at a man who should be a two-dimensional stain.

Enoch was dazed, more from the shock of what had happened than anything else. But as he stood, I saw that he was gripping his side. *Broken ribs,* I mused. *So he can be hurt.*

"Let's get out of here and disappear. If we're lucky, we'll never see that ex-archangel again," I said, giving Enoch one last look. He just stared back at me with a maniacal smile on his face that I took as a sign that our little love affair was truly over. Like him trying to strangle me to death wasn't enough of a sign.

The gloves were off now. I could see that in his eyes. No more banter. No more trying to persuade me to be the love of his life. He had underestimated the *And they knew each other* part of our relationship. Should we meet again, he would play for keeps.

Best course of action: get rid of the Soul Jar and make sure he never saw me again.

As if reading my mind, he pointed at his lips—evidently his stalking was so detailed that he knew all about my ability to read lips —and mouthed, *"Katrina Darling, you haven't seen the last of me."*

Normally a cliché like that would have me rolling my eyes, but seeing the deadly serious look on his lips made me and my newly reinstated soul shiver.

I slammed on the accelerator, and as we drove past him, he made no attempt to follow or catch us. At least we had one small thing going for us this day.

"Where are we going, milady?" Deirdre asked.

"We need to get out of Dodge."

"Dodge?"

Oh yeah, I was back with my fae *I don't know human slang* roommate. Sighing and not in the mood to give her our usual 'being human' lesson, I said, "We need to get off the island. But first, we have to take Egya to a vet."

Egya snickered before licking me on the face.

11

THAT VOODOO THAT YOU DO
SO WELL

I drove the ridiculous bus to Kokusai Dori, the main street that signified the center of Okinawa's capital, Naha. There, I found the very same parking center where two Nio statues had almost ended my life only days earlier. But two *gaijin* and a hyena wouldn't get far in a dented bus before some enterprising policeman pulled us over. Best to abandon the bus, and this complex was the only place I could think of to do so.

Getting out of the bus, I looked over at the spot where I thought I was finally going to say goodbye to this GoneGod World and sighed. "Ever feel like it's one step forward, two steps back?"

I had muttered that out loud, seeking a wee bit of comfort from my companions. But given that Egya was a dog and Deirdre was fae, I really wished that my laments had been silent.

"No, milady," Deirdre said with all the seriousness of a heart attack. "Did the evil man cast a confusion spell on you?"

Deirdre took my silence not as the intended *You got to be kidding me,* and said, "Milady, we are very much moving forward. Watch." The changeling warrior took several steps forward before realizing that she had walked away from—and in the opposite direction of—the exit.

She'd need to walk back to me—in other words, backward—to get out of the parking complex.

I waited for her to make her way back to me. "See what I mean?"

Deirdre nodded. "Another human expression that is not meant to be literal."

"Indubitably," I said as we walked to the exit.

Egya was relieving himself on a nearby car.

"Egya, what are you doing?"

He finished his business before trotting over to me.

"I'm going to give you the benefit of the doubt and assume that was you literally throwing Enoch off our scent, right? The owner of that car goes home, Enoch tracks us by scent, follows said owner, thus buying us some time?"

Egya paused, cocked his head to one side in that way dogs do when thinking, and nodded. Given how long that all took, I knew he hadn't thought of any of that and just needed to go.

"Genius," Deirdre said.

"Oh yes," I said, rigourously petting him behind his ears. "What a good dog. What a good, good dog."

↔

I hated doing this, especially given what happened the last time, but I only knew one place where we could go to get help. Kenji's izakaya. Well, that's not true—we could find Jean and ask for military help. But given his commander wanted to basically enlist me as an indentured servant, making me go on black-ops missions for the U.S. military, I thought he'd be Plan B.

And Plan C would be Keiko. But given how badass Enoch was, I didn't want to bring him to Blue's doorstep. I couldn't do that to them.

That meant that Kenji was Plan A. Plan A sucked. The last time I visited him, the place was attacked by monstrous statues, Kenji was arrested by the U.S. military and we almost died.

I'd definitely made a huge withdrawal from the Kat-Kenji emotional bank.

Still, he was an old friend. And a good person ... well, Other. He'd help us. He had to.

I was about to go through the curtain that served as a door when Egya grabbed my hand.

Given that he was a dog, it was more of a bite. A wet, disgusting bite.

I withdrew my hand. "What?"

Egya motioned his head; he was trying to show me something. I considered going through the whole, "What is it, boy?" routine when I actually followed his gaze to what he was warning me about.

On the edge of Kenji's door was what looked like a mezuzah, except the symbols weren't the traditional Hebrew inscription, but rather a teeny-tiny pyramid with an eye in it.

The Eye of Providence. More like the ever-watching eye of Sauron. It was the celestial version of a hidden camera. So Enoch was watching this place just in case I got away. Which I had. Which meant that he was a planner. And a planner like him would also be watching my Plans B and C.

Shit.

There was literally nowhere for me to go.

↔

We walked away from the Kenji's place back to the main street, where the generally human population looked at the giant hyena with trepidation. I ducked into the closest woman's clothing store and bought a pink hat and a large kariyushi-wear shirt. "Here, put these on," I said to Egya.

The giant hyena refused.

"Look around us," I said. "People are scared of you. We need to cute-ify you so that we don't add 'in trouble with the police' to our long list of crap to deal with." I bent down to help him get the shirt on. It was harder than you'd think, but with only a little rip on the seam, we managed to get it around his body. I put on the hat, tying it around his neck. "Besides, pink suits you."

And as we continued to walk down the street, I noted that the looks of fear were replaced with confused looks of amusement.

Baby steps. Baby steps ...

↔

So, we were out of friends, had no place to go, no vehicle to ride away in, stuck out like sore thumbs in a country that generally took notice of two foreign women with a giant dog and were being hunted by a guy who had access to the largest magical arsenal I'd ever seen.

At least I had my ATM card on me. Thank the GoneGods for small miracles.

Which was more than I could say for my passport. That was still firmly in the hands of Okinawan airport security, which, given that Enoch had basically enchanted the place, meant that he had it.

I imagined him perving over my passport picture and cringed.

"Where do we go? Where do we go now?" I sang to myself to the tune of "Sweet Child of Mine."

"Milady?" Deirdre looked at me like I was losing my mind, which I very well could have been.

"It's just that we're out of options. I have no idea what or where we could go. We literally need a miracle, and right now miracles are in short supply—"

And as if my prayers were being answered, a miracle did happen.

A dirty, low-down, horrible, terribly ironic miracle in the form of a picture. A poster, actually, of an event that was to take place in Okinawa later that day.

And who was the star of the show? The very same dark elf who just happened to be my ex-boyfriend.

Yaay ...

PART III

INTERMISSION:

Long, long ago, Enoch was a pious man. A unique one, too, who helped the angels in their civil war.

Back then, some rebellious upstarts wanted to usurp God's power. Like such a thing was possible. They rebelled. They fought. But they were smart enough to know that they could not win a war in Heaven. So they fell to Earth and used its lush, primitive groups to fight.

Enoch watched as angels stabbed and clawed at each other. And seeing right from wrong, chose a side—the winning side.

He chose God's side.

The frail human risked everything to save as many angels' lives as he could. And his bravery did not go unnoticed.

He was taken up to Heaven—only one of three humans to gain such a privilege without dying to do so. There, he stood before a pleased God who demanded further service. For Enoch had witnessed the battles and judged wisely. He would become exactly that: witness and judge.

But a human cannot preside over lesser gods and angels. So God made him an angel. And not just any angel ... a great archangel with powers that would rival even the archangel Michael.

And thus Enoch was transformed into an archangel of the highest order. He was given a new name—Metatron— and was tasked to judge over the gods and angels when they meddled in human affairs. His sole purpose was to punish those who went too far. Which, given the providence of the gods, was quite far indeed.

↔

And so he took to his role. Judging and punishing gods and angels, alike.

His last judgement was over Lyssa, the goddess of madness. She had turned the great Theban hero Actaeon into a stag before infecting his team of hunting dogs with rabies. Then she laughed as Actaeon ran for his life, the hunter now the hunted, only to be cornered and dismembered by the hounds.

The centaur Chiron had trained Actaeon, and brought a case against Lyssa, arguing that her cruelty went beyond the providence of gods. But in the end, Chiron had no case. Actaeon had stumbled upon the goddess Artemis bathing in a river and gazed upon her naked body. It was well within the rights of the gods to kill the man, even if he had done so by accident.

With Metatron's judgment complete, he sought to take his leave, but was interrupted by the three Sisters of Fate. They had come to watch over the proceedings. Why? They already knew the outcome. The Great Tapestry had shown them exactly what Metatron would decide.

In unison, the three sisters spoke as if one. "Witness," they chorused, "we have something for you to see."

Another case to preside over?

As if sensing his question, they answered, "The gods chose to meddle, and such meddling will end all. Come see for yourself. The tapestry calls for you."

Wary to listen, Metatron knew he should consult God—or, at the very least, a higher angel—before following creatures such as the Fates. But alas, Metatron had not fully freed himself from his human vices, and the vice of curiosity demanded that he follow.

↔

Metatron enters the Fates' chambers, where the three sisters stand over their incredible tapestry.

The first sister taps Metatron on the shoulder. The archangel whirls around, his eyes engulfed with fury. How dare this lesser creature touch him? The impudence—the arrogance! To touch one such as him without permission is a bold act that even the gods would be wary of doing. He would be within his rights to end her existence here and now.

But then he remembers the tapestry, and understands that this Fate has nothing to fear. She has already seen her future, and it does not include being torn asunder by him.

He cannot help but laugh. To know your own future … to know the futures of all … such insight must be both a curse and a boon.

"What is it that you wish to show me, Sisters?" Metatron demands.

"This," the three sisters say in unison. Three brittle fingers point to the corner of their quilt, but instead of seeing the antiquated intertwining of all living beings' fates, it is black … dark. Empty.

"We have woven the Threads of Destiny," echoes one of them.

"Seen the fates of all," murmurs the second.

"And everything—everyone—comes to the same moment. There in the corner resides the empty future of all."

"A fateless future."

"One without destiny."

"Or purpose."

"Or meaning."

"Is that the End of Days?" Metatron muses. He has read the scriptures; he knows that the gods have always planned an end of sorts. But that end was for their creations. Their *mortal* creations. The promise of life everlasting for their favored children always remained.

But if he is to understand this tapestry correctly, then the End of Days will be the end of all.

He speaks this conclusion out loud. "If the gods choose to end everything, that is their right."

"Spoken like the pious whipping boy …"

"… that the angels are."

"You dare," Metatron bellows, his anger rising as the scent of brimstone and sulfur attend his intent. "Apologize! Apologize, or the universe will be forced to continue without the likes of you."

"Ahh, angels," the three sisters say.

"Such confidence."

"Such arrogance."

"Such a contradiction …"

"… for one as powerful as you to always be so willing to"—the sister pauses, as if searching for the word—"to follow."

Metatron's anger grows, and he takes a step forward as he manifests a sword made entirely of flames. As soon as the blade appears, a protective, sea-green halo surrounds Metatron. He is prepared for battle, and the form he takes is fearsome.

But the sisters show no fear.

The sisters know full well what he is capable of. They know what he is willing to do, and yet they goad him still. Given their own divine powers, Metatron understands that he is in great danger, for the Sisters of Fate do not fear him.

They do not fear him because they know he will not kill them. They already know how this conversation ends. And given his anger and willingness to end them, this can only mean one of two things: either he will be subdued, or he will be convinced.

Lifting his blade in a defensive manner, he looks around. There is nothing here to harm him. And with the halo, he is armored with God's protection. No charm, illusion or enchantment can possess him now.

Which means that the sisters do not seek to subdue him. They mean to convince him.

Metatron knows he should take to the sky to retreat and re-evaluate. But even though he has shed his mortal coil, has become an archangel of great power and the leader of the Eighth Order of Angels, he still possess perhaps the greatest and most deadly of human traits: curiosity.

Sheathing his sword, he points at the darkened spot of the tapestry. "Show me what you wish me to know. And waste no more of my time, Sisters. Speak plainly and speak quickly."

"As you wish," the sisters say.

"We will not speak at all, but rather let the words of the gods speak for themselves," says the first sister.

"For when they abandon us, their message is simple," says the second.

"*Thank you for believing in us, but it is not enough ...*" says the third.

12

DARK ELVES, EX-BOYFRIENDS AND MOTIVATIONAL SPEAKERS

*W*hen I was a young vampire of eighty years, I fell in love for the first time. His name was Aldermemnon, but he was Aldie to me. I met him one evening while hunting in a local graveyard just outside of Prague.

I liked hunting in graveyards, not so much because I was an evil creature of the night, but because those places tended to be quiet and relatively unoccupied. Usually you'd find one or two stragglers around, lovers on a walk celebrating their life-filled joy while exploring the finality of their existence, a vagrant looking for somewhere to sleep … a mourner who wandered there to speak to someone no longer around.

Also, because it was a graveyard, once you were done with the body you could just dump it into some open grave.

Hunting in a graveyard was easy pickings, the vampires' equivalent of fast food. Quick, cheap and you didn't have to clean up after yourself.

I had just finished draining an old man who had come to sit by his wife's grave. He was so overcome with grief that he didn't even try to run away, instead welcoming the death I brought.

Once he was gone—hopefully to join his wife in the After (the gods were still around back then, so as long as he got into the same heaven or hell, they'd find each other)—I heard a slow clapping from behind me.

I turned to find out what, or rather who, was the source of the noise, but I couldn't see anyone. That was strange. I was a vampire, after all. With my heightened senses, I could see in the dark just as easily as one could see in broad daylight. My hearing and sense of smell were attuned to find whatever I was looking for ... especially if what I was looking for had a heartbeat.

And presumably, whoever clapped had a heartbeat.

But I saw no one. Just the statues and tombstones littering this place.

Shaking it off as a trick of my mind, I'd stood to leave when I heard a voice—soft and pleasant, but somehow still firm and confident—say, "I admire your technique. Subtle, quick, but still full of joy. Well, joy for you, at least. That said, I am fairly sure he whispered, 'Thank you' just before the end."

The voice felt as though it came from everywhere at once, which didn't really help me pinpoint where my admirer was standing.

"He did." I scanned my surroundings. Not being able to see the creature unsettled me. It had been over eighty years since anything had been able to sneak up on me.

"So perhaps joy for you both, then?"

I still couldn't find the damn creature, but the fact that it hadn't revealed itself to me meant it was playing with me. Good thing I knew how to play, too. "Why not come out of the shadows so that we may enjoy each other, too?"

A chuckle. "Very good, young vampire. A bit of wit. A bit of humor. And humor does mask fear. For, after all, one cannot be scared and laughing at the same time."

"Not unless you're insane."

"Not unless you're insane," he mused. "Yes, I suppose that is correct."

"So, will you come out of the shadows and play?" I touched the upper button of my blouse in a suggestive way.

"I would, but I'm not in the shadows."

"Then where are you?"

"Right in front of you."

I stared directly into the space in front of me, but all I saw was a statue of a young boy holding an urn spilling stone liquid over its edge. Flowers poured out amongst the water, which made it quite beautiful. Of course, I had seen dozens like it; this was a typical statue for graveyards in this region and era.

Still, the statue was considerably larger than normal, and—

Without hesitation, I lunged forward and punched the stone face as hard as I could.

My fist met hard rock, and my hand exploded with pain.

That shouldn't have happened. Don't get me wrong—as a human, punching a statue with everything you've got is bound to break your hand. That's to be expected. But as a vampire? My fist should have sailed through that stone like I was punching a piñata, except instead of candy bursting out, either the statue would have been reduced to rubble or—following my theory that this statue was alive—brains.

Neither happened.

I staggered back, cradling my hand. "What the—?"

The statue's face contorted into a smile as the creature stepped off the pedestal. As soon as his feet touched the ground, his stone exterior turned into dark, almond-colored skin and his clothing became flexible, just like fabric should.

"Who are you?" In my relatively short life (well, short for an immortal), I had only ever encountered other vampires.

I'd never met something else. And here I was, standing in front of a being who was clearly not human.

I'm not proud of what I did next, but it was the only thing I could think of. I crossed myself. As in, spectacles, testicles, wallet and watch, as my lips uttered a prayer. Hey, I was a Highlands girl who had gone to church every Sunday until the day I died. Some habits die hard.

"Tat, tat, tat." He lifted an admonishing finger. "None of that." He gave me the warmest, most inviting smile, and I immediately felt safe in his presence.

And his eyes ... Oh, his eyes were the perfect shade of stormy gray, like they housed an entire horizon frothing with turmoil and beauty.

This creature was exquisite.

But he was more than that. I understood beauty. Hell, I used beauty when hunting; vampires are imbued with an unnatural allure ourselves. It helps when drawing in prey.

This creature was beyond exquisite. He was something else entirely.

He approached me, hand outstretched. "I am sorry about your hand. But that was stoneskin, milady. You never punch someone with stoneskin cast on them. It can only lead to ... well ..." He touched my broken hand.

Shit. He'd touched my broken hand, which meant that I'd let him get close enough to attack. Stupid, stupid, stupid!

But he didn't attack. Instead, that gentle touch instantly healed my hand.

"What? How? ... What are you?"

He looked genuinely confused that I didn't know what he was. Hurt, almost. "You really don't know, do you?"

I shook my head.

"My dear, for a vampire, you are woefully lacking in knowledge of the underworld and what it has to offer."

I considered being insulted, but I was too busy swooning. My god, he was perfect.

"Come, dear vampire." He stretched out his hand. "Come, let me show you a whole new world." He used that line on me centuries before Aladdin said the same thing to Princess Jasmine. And as a young vampire who had just realized that myths—Other myths—were real, let me tell you: it worked.

Eat a man alive, it worked.

↔

. . .

Staring at that poster, I was flooded with memories of Aldie. The world of fae and myths wasn't the only thing he had showed me during the years that followed.

I had been a virgin when I met him all those years ago. I wasn't a virgin when I left him. Made me think of that Disney song and what it's really about. I mean, think about it.

I can open your eyes
Take you wonder by wonder
Over sideways and under
On a magic carpet ride

People shagged on carpets long before there *were* shag carpets. And as for the unbelievable sights, the indescribable feeling ... and all that soaring, tumbling, and freewheeling promised in the song? Well, you get the picture.

(If I just ruined Aladdin for you, my apologies. But let's be honest, Disney was filled with double entendres, subtext and read-between-the-lines adult content. I mean ... "Hakuna Matata," "Can You Feel the Love Tonight" ... "For the First Time in Forever?" Masturbation, losing your virginity and, oh yeah, losing your virginity. There's a theme here, people ... Then again, it might just be me.)

↔

Disney's outlet for adolescent exploration of sex aside, the point is that Aldie was my first, and him being an immortal fae, he was one hell of a first.

"Milady. *Milady.*"

"Huh?" I looked up dreamily from the poster.

"You are singing," Deirdre said with genuine concern. "In all the time I have known you, you have never once spontaneously broken into song. And yet you have done it twice in the last five minutes."

"Was I?" I said hazily.

"Indeed. Something about going from wonder to wonder, dazzling places and shooting stars. Despite your propensity for airing your thoughts, I have never known you to sing them. Are you possessed? Has Enoch enchanted you? Are you going to sing everything now?"

Deirdre was in full warrior mode, scanning the crowd for any sign of Enoch. Egya, on the other hand, was chuckling as he gave me knowing looks. I had told him about my dark elf ex, and the hyena was no dummy. He knew exactly who this guy was. Damn hyenas.

"That's from *Aladdin,*" I said to Deirdre.

"The mongrel who enslaved one of the jinn?"

"No, the olive-skinned guy from the movies."

Deirdre's eyes narrowed in obvious confusion.

"Disney, Deirdre. Disney. Come on, if we survive this, I'm going to show you a whole new world, and I need you to interpret that with a PG-rating in mind."

"Milady?"

"Never mind … Let's go."

↔

I explained everything to Deirdre and Egya as we walked to Naha's conference center, where the event was taking place. The event that Aldie had organized. The event he was throwing in Okinawa tonight. As we approached, I saw huge posters of the dark elf standing with confidence and the biggest, most inviting smile on his face.

Giant screens outside the venue played snippets of the event on repeat: Aldie ziplining over the audience and onto stage as fireworks went off; Aldie walking through the aisles, talking with the audience; Aldie triumphantly pumping his fist in the air.

And interlaced throughout the ad, slogans flashed. Slogans like: *Embrace your Destiny. Awaken the Sleeping Giant Within. Find Your Inner Banshee.*

My ex-boyfriend was a self-help guru, and judging from the crowd of Others eagerly standing in line, he was more than just a wannabe.

Aldie was the Tony Robbins of mythical self-help. And just as I thought that, a picture of Aldie standing next to Tony Robbins popped up on the screen.

"Finally embracing your destiny, Aldie?" I muttered as Egya snickered.

13

YOU NEED TO TAKE A SWIM IN LAKE YOU

*G*etting in was easier than I'd thought. Given that the event was obviously sold out, I was sure I'd have to bribe some attendant or sneak in through a back door. But as soon as we entered the ticketing area, one bright-eyed sphinx wearing a hat that read *Make Your Mortal Life Immortal* said, "Hurry up, the exotic animals need to be backstage and ready immediately."

Humph, a smiling sphinx who didn't speak in riddles ... I knew Aldie could change a person, but that was something else.

I glanced down at Egya. He was still wearing his pink hat and his kariyushi shirt ... and looking positively depressed about it.

"Hold on," I whispered to him. "This is just to get us inside. Then we'll free you from your *kawaii* adornments."

He gave a snort as we walked through the doors. Evidently he didn't believe me.

The sphinx led us backstage, where a whole bunch of what should be wild animals mulled about with their various trainers. There was a tiger, a llama, three puffins, a white-faced capuchin, an ocelot ... and now a hyena, all backstage.

The sphinx pointed to the back. "Who's his handler?"

"Handler?"

"Which one of you is going to take him on stage?"

I lifted an unsure hand.

The sphinx eyed Deirdre. "And who are you?"

"I am Deirdre of the clan—"

"She's security," I said before she could give the sphinx her entire lineage dating back to the dawn of time. Never ask a fae who they are unless you have about a day and a half to waste ... They make Biblical genealogy seem reasonable.

"I see." The sphinx gave Egya a look. "A bit of a handful?"

I grinned. Egya groaned. And Deirdre, who wasn't very big on subterfuge, nodded with total sincerity.

"Fine ... just be ready," the sphinx said, walking away.

↔

Egya and I stood backstage as the show commenced ... Or rather, I should say the spectacle commenced, because that was exactly what it was. It started with the thumping base of "We Are the Champions," except instead of Freddie Mercury crying out "the world," the speakers (and audience) cried out, "*our* world."

Small distinction, but so very self-help*ish*, and Aldie*ish*, too. Then the stage before us erupted with fire, but not the typical blasts of fire you'd see at a rock concert. These were fireballs that manifested like exploding stars on the stage.

Someone was burning time to create that effect. Someone was losing valuable minutes of their life just for this audience's amusement. And from the reaction of the crowd, I knew that was part of the point. The audience was mostly Others ... Others who limited their expressions of magic in this godless world because it cost them life.

I thought back to the fireballs that had manifested out of thin air, just like they had been conjured by magic. To use magic was to burn time. Aldie implied that he was sacrificing a bit of himself for them. That he was giving his life for them.

Then I thought back to Aldie's picture. A bit of gray in his goatee, slight wrinkles on his face. He had aged far more than an elf should in four years.

I don't know what infuriated me more ... that he manipulated their emotions, or that I understood exactly why he did. In a world where they had been abandoned by their gods, discarded as worthless and unworthy, Aldie gave a piece of himself to them.

It is no understatement that to a once immortal being, death is terrifying. It is terrifying to humans, but at least we're born knowing that we will one day die. For Others, their birth came with the promise of forever. And now that their forever was gone, the threat of something they hadn't yet come to accept as a given was crushing. Others rarely burn time, even a second of it, unless they are trying to escape immediate death.

For them to burn time otherwise is out of great personal cost. And should they do so for you, then you must understand the gift they bestow on you. For you.

To burn a second is to invite death. And as I thought back on all the times Others had burned time for someone else, it humbled me.

'Deirdre, Mergen, Cassandra, Aelfric and Remi ... they've all burned time to help others. We do not deserve them.'

Egya grunted in agreement.

Another fireball, followed by three more. Aldie wasn't just burning a bit of time—he was giving a lot of it. His message was clear: You are worth it. You are worthy.

The cynical part of me wanted to temper such offerings with the fact that they were paying him to make all this. But that was tempered by the realization that Aldie could have created a spectacle without burning any time, and it would have been just as grand.

He was giving up a part of himself on purpose. This wasn't the selfish narcissist I remembered.

To see it done here and now, and so blatantly, too—the sacrifice for the spectacle—well, even I was moved. And I was just about as cynical toward Aldie as humanly possible.

A black arrow big enough to slay a dragon flew from the back of the audience, striking the stump of a massive oak tree that probably took a couple of giants to hoist on stage. The arrow was tethered to a rope that hung taut from the back of the stage.

As soon as the arrow embedded itself in the hard wood, Aldie ziplined over the sea of adoring fans, landing on the stage with a superhero tumble that would have made Black Panther cringe with CGI envy.

GoneGodDamn! I forgot how graceful elves were.

And just when I thought Aldie's entrance couldn't be any more over the top, he did a black flip before landing *not* on his feet like a normal acrobat, but rather—no friggin' way—his pinky finger.

Boy oh boy, Aldie had learned some new tricks.

OK, maybe not as selfish as he once was, but still the planet-sized narcissist, I see.

Pushing off with his one finger, Aldie finally got to his feet, turning around and around with arms outstretched as he soaked up the audience's adulation.

Seeing his face for the first time, I saw that the impossibly youthful face he'd once had was replaced with one that possessed not worry lines, but wrinkles that screamed wisdom. Just like the pictures, he had little flecks of gray in his beard, far grayer than four years of mortal aging should have given him. A small part of me had doubted that Aldie was the one actually burning time to create those fireballs, but finally seeing him here, I knew for sure.

It wasn't someone else burning magic ... it was Aldie.

He *was* literally giving a little bit of himself with every show.

↔

Aldie stood perfectly still on the stage in that way I've only known the fae to be able to do. So still that they basically become statues. If his energy had been infectious, then so was his complete stillness.

The audience slowly began to mirror him, their cries of adulation quieting under the weight of Aldie's tranquility. Mutterings turned to whispers that blossomed into complete silence. The sea of moving bodies bore the tension of undisturbed water.

But it was more than silence and stillness. There were no soft murmurs typical of such a large space—no creaks, gusts of wind, those indefinable sounds you'd hear in a full auditorium. In the absolute silence, I listened for breathing and heard none, and I wondered if everyone truly held their breath or if this was more time being burnt to give the illusion of perfect nothingness.

I honestly could not tell, but sensing my own held breath, I wondered how long we all would stay like this until some of us started passing out from lack of oxygen.

A part of me wanted to start laughing, to pierce the overblown grandeur with my mockery. But another, more evolved part of me knew that was just my discomfort at being connected to so many all at once. It was unnatural for thousands of lost souls to be united like this.

And this foreign feeling both gave me the peace of belonging and discomfort of being a part of something that I ... what? ... shouldn't be a part of? Didn't deserve?

No. *Part of something I wasn't doing enough for ...*

That last thought hit me in a way that only suddenly realized truth could, but before I could explore that feeling, I shook my head, chasing away the severity of my thoughts. This was a self-help seminar. It was fifty shades of self-affirmation bullshit, and just because I was thrown off-kilter by Aldie's presence, I wasn't about to let myself spiral into whatever self-loathing crap was swimming around in my head.

Now I really was going to laugh, to pierce this facade with a chuckle. But before I could, Aldie beat me to it with four simple words that, instead of being uplifting, only pulled me further down into the depths.

"We do not belong."

A strange beginning to a self-help pep talk.

Aldie took a step forward, his hands outstretched like he was trying to embrace the entire auditorium.

"We do not belong," he repeated.

Doubling down, eh?

"We are the alien invaders, the barbarian hordes at the gate, the unwanted masses at the doorstep of a world that is not ready or capable of having us. It's in our name: Others. As in, not them."

OK, now I'm getting depressed. I thought these things were all 'Live your potential,' 'Awaken the giant within,' 'Love yourself and the world will, too.'

"So let me say it again: We do not belong. Not a single one of us. I need you to understand this, because that is the truth. We do not belong. And the moment you truly understand that will be the moment you stop feeling sorry for yourself ..."

Here we go.

"... stop expecting this GoneGod World to help you out and ..."

Give it to us, Aldie.

"... start getting off your ass and doing something about it."

There we go! Hold on, folks, we're going full self-help now.

"Did you ever expect humans—humans!—to welcome us with open arms? Come on, Others! You knew better than that. Humans do not even like their own kind, so why would they embrace ones such as us? Look at my funny ears." He pretended to prick his pointy ear with an "Ouch." The audience chuckled.

"Or your ridiculous eye." He pointed at a cyclops. "Do you save extra at Spec-savers because you only need one lens?"

Lame, but the audience chuckled their approval.

"And what about you?" He pointed to the middle of the audience, and the giant jumbotron screens focused on a kappa. "You look like an extra in *Super Mario Bros.*"

The bipedal turtle slapped his shell with chortles of laughter.

"None of us belong, because we don't look like them ... and they don't like anything or anyone that doesn't look like them. I mean, look at their most popular version of God. He made them in his image. Or perhaps they made Him in their image." He rubbed his chin in mocking reflection. "So I guess Anubis, Ganesh, Raijin and Baron Samedi didn't get the memo. Then again, they all left, so ..."

He let those last words hang in the air.

"We may be different, but that doesn't make us less. It doesn't make us unworthy. But it does mean we have to work twice as hard, twice as long and twice as diligently before they'll finally accept us ...

"So, my fellow Others of the GoneGod World, are you ready to embrace your destiny?"

If the audience was energized before, they became positively electric after that little gem. It took every ounce of my willpower to not roll my eyes, and even then I didn't have the strength to hold in the give-me-a-break sigh that escaped my judgmental lips.

Aldie was always a showman, but this was over the top, even for him. Then again, he was burning time to make these extravaganzas extravangadizize.

And as for genuine, I wasn't sure. Aldie had always been the over-the-top optimist who could get a death row inmate excited about tomorrow while they strapped him to the chair. His gregarious nature made Bacchus look shy. He was an extroverts' Superman.

But being so out there also meant that he lost interest in things just when you thought it was getting good. I mean, the bastard lost interest in me after only eighty years.

I know eighty years might sound like a long time, especially now that we're all mortal, but eighty years to someone who lives forever is barely a summer fling.

Of course, back then there was a lot of pressure for us to break up. The entire UnSeelie Court was literally against us. A half-breed like me and a prince of the fae was a big no-no. Fae are many things, and arrogant is probably at the top of that list. They saw my human nature as disgusting and my demonic nature as animalistic. To them, I was no better than a chimpanzee.

So imagine a human and a chimpanzee rocking up to city hall, demanding a marriage certificate, and you'll start to get a sense of how they viewed us.

Not that Aldie cared. He defied his realm, relishing in the scandal. At first I saw it as romantic. It wasn't until much later that I realized it was part of his narcissistic nature. Better to be talked about and reviled than ignored.

And Aldie hated being ignored.

Of course, it didn't help that his parents were overachieving, domineering crusaders who were credited with negotiating peace between the Seelie and UnSeelie courts. I mean, there were history books written about them.

But it was more than that. Fae, like most Others, cannot have children on their own. They must petition their gods for a child. As a reward for brokering peace, Danu—goddess of fertility, wisdom, wind and the Celtic people—granted them Aldie, the only child to be born in the UnSeelie Court in a millennium. A lot of expectations were pinned to him.

Because of his intelligence, grace and charisma, those expectations weren't just from the world outside him. Aldie had those expectations of himself.

Trouble was, when the expectation is that of general greatness, and there's nothing defining what that greatness could be ... it becomes impossible to fulfill.

And seeing him prance around the stage, inspiring hope in these hopeless Others, I wondered if he had finally found the greatness he so desperately desired.

I watched Aldie prance around the stage, hugging chupacabras, slapping the backs of banshees, high-fiving carbuncles, and I couldn't help but wonder when he'd lose interest in this crowd.

Given how they hung on his every word, I hoped he wouldn't. Those Others looked up to him, full of something very rare in the GoneGod World ... hope.

I felt a hand push my shoulder. It was the sphinx, gesturing for me to get on stage. The other animal handlers were already entering the stage, and I heard Aldie say, "We are different. But there is so much difference already on this planet. Take a look at the eagle, the llama, the platypus." As he spoke, me and Egya were being pushed out onto the stage. "And it's not just them. Join me in welcoming the zoo of the bizarre and—"

"—Kat?"

"Ahh, Hi Aldie," I said.

Gulp.

14
BACKSTAGE ISN'T AS GLAMOROUS AS YOU'D THINK

"*K*at," he repeated.

"Ahh, hey," I said again. Egya's hyena form snickered in an all-too-human way.

The audience, still and confused, waited for Aldie to do or say something. But instead he just stared at me, his eyes narrowing as he tried to comprehend what was happening. I suddenly felt very selfish for bursting in on him this way. A part of me wanted to give him a wee jab for how he'd ended things. Payback served publicly.

I didn't consider the thousands of Others staring at us now. Nor did I consider how the sight of me would affect him. After all, he broke up with me. He ended it in the most callous, hurtful way imaginable, and I figured that because he didn't care for me then, seeing me now would just throw him off.

What I didn't expect were his stormy gray eyes softening as he stared at me that way he used to when we … um … how does Ella Fitzgerald put it? Made whoopee.

I also didn't expect my own heart to flutter under his gaze. Damn, he was beautiful … but it was more than that. My heart also chorused with a thousand memories of when things were good. I wanted to go to him—no, that wasn't right. I wanted to go back to a time when things were good between us. I wanted to go back to him.

My brain, however, managed to jump in and remind my stupid, traitorous heart what Aldie did to me. *How* he did it.

That was enough.

I gave Aldie that smile I used when saying, "Nice try." That look used to send him into a rage, and I figured it would wake him up from whatever fugue state he was in now. But it didn't. He just sighed, and I saw that his hands trembled ever so slightly.

Shit.

OK, time for me to get a little less subtle. "Hello everyone," I said. Not that anyone who wasn't sitting in the front row could hear me. I wasn't miked up.

I looked around for a microphone, and the only one I could see was currently pinned to Aldie's shirt. I stepped forward, and leaning close to his chest, said, "Hi everyone. Sorry to burst in like this, but I thought I'd surprise Aldie here. We're old friends."

It was awkward leaning in so close to him like that. It was even more awkward being so close to his chest and trying to make whatever eye contact I could with the audience.

Hearing me say that must have done the trick, because Aldie caught himself, remembering where he was ... and who he was in front of. He cleared his throat. "That is true, but incomplete." He turned to the audience. "And what is a half-truth but a ..." He lifted his hands like the conductor in an orchestra, and the audience chorused out, *"lie."*

"And lies are good for ..."

"Nothing but pain."

"And there is enough of that in this GoneGod World without us adding to it. I made a promise to you, but more importantly to myself, to always be the best version of me. Now, if I were immortal and an endless parade of tomorrows were still laid out before me, I might make some quip, dismiss the gravity of this reunion. After all, when there is always a sea of time to run from such encounters, why does anything hold importance? But there is no more time to turn the significant into a distant memory. And without that time, the only thing we can do is face it."

He turned to me, angling his body so that the cameras picked up his face. Always the showman. With eyes that expressed endless empathy, he said, "And so to complete the truth, we were friends, but also lovers. And that affair ended so very, very horribly. How fitting. For what do I always say?"

"Your fate did not end with the gods."

"And it seems that my fate is to face the horribleness of my past." He sighed, looking back at me. "I suspect that such an experience will be something I shall share with you all."

A chuckle sounded from the audience.

"But first thing's first. I promised you an event you will not forget, and although I believe I have delivered on this already, this life-changing seminar isn't over. Not nearly." Aldie turned to me. Getting on one knee, he took my hand. "My dear Katrina, as you can imagine, your presence is distracting. If you don't mind waiting for me backstage, I'll be out soon."

I nodded. "I waited for you for a couple hundred years. What's a few more hours?"

"Ouch," Aldie said to the laughing audience. "I'd say that was uncalled for, but that would be a lie. That was very much called for. Very much indeed."

↔

The sphinx who had earlier mistaken me for an animal handler escorted me backstage, where she insisted I hand over Egya to Deirdre. "Wait for me here," I said as I followed the sphinx to Aldie's dressing room.

Once inside, the sphinx unceremoniously huffed before waddling away. "I'm sorry," I called after her. It was the least I could do.

Alone I looked around the room. It was surprisingly bare given how lavish the Aldie I knew liked to live. Sparse with only a dressing mirror, some makeup and three changes of clothes.

An open suitcase sat on the couch. In it was a hair dryer, some spare clothes, sunglasses and the book, *The 7 Habits of Highly Effective People*.

Next to it was another book with Aldie's face on it: *The 13 Rules for Being Mortal*.

Oh brother, he was an author, too.

It was probably full of useless tripe. Then again, I did have a couple hours to kill before he wrapped up so, I picked it up, looked at the ridiculous smile on his face and groaned as I opened it up.

(If you'd like a summary of Aldie's book, click here and join Mortality Bites FB Group. Aldie's principles can be found inside!)

↔

First I skimmed his book. Then I read it. Short, but surprisingly good. And not just for Others. For anyone mortal, really. Practical advice, moving stories ... there were even a few stories about his ex-girlfriend (well, technically his ex-*vampire* ex-girlfriend. But so many clauses were a mouthful, so a forgivable omission, given that my demonic past wasn't the point).

I had just finished reading about habit nine—Time Well-Burnt is Time Well-Spent—when I heard applause.

The changing room had been fairly insulated from the auditorium, but I still heard the explosion of cheers and clapping that told me Aldie had just finished his grand finale. I took a deep breath as I waited for my ex-boyfriend and the first person I ever truly loved to make it to the dressing room.

I heard the tapping of shoes on linoleum coming from the hallway. The steps echoed in a rhythm that implied someone was running, and before I could slow the frantic rush of my heart, Aldie burst into the room, slamming the door behind him.

"Before you say anything, I just—"

Aldie pulled me in close, kissing me with every fiber of his being and, at that moment, I'd like to say that I remembered Justin. Remembered that I had a boyfriend—a very hurt boyfriend—who was probably wondering where I was.

But Justin was the last thing on my mind. Hell, breathing was the last thing on my mind. All I knew at that moment was how warm and safe it felt to be in his arms. The outside world, with all its warring and squabbling, maniacal, wannabe gods and lost mortals, death and life … none of it meant anything.

All I knew was Aldie. And that felt great.

After what felt like an eternity, Aldie pulled away, grinning at me with those impossibly deep dimples accenting his smile.

It took me a moment to remember why I was here, but the memory of Enoch's little bag of tricks jolted me back to reality. I cleared my throat. "As I was saying, before you say anything …"

"And I said nothing."

I touched my lips. "I think you said plenty. Now, if you'll hear me out …" I began turning away so that I didn't have to look at him as I asked—nay, begged—for his help.

But Aldie was in front of me in a flash. I swear he must have burned a bit of time to get in front of me so fast. "No. After all these centuries, you have found your way back to me. Whatever it is, whatever you need, the answer is yes. I only have one condition."

"I'm not sleeping with you." I immediately regretted saying that. Aldie may have been a dark elf from the UnSeelie Court, but he was not the kind of person to ever use his position to get what he wanted.

He looked down at me with his perfect, cloudy gray eyes, and the storm within them seemed to grow at my suggestion.

"Sorry," I said. "It's been a long day. Hell, a long re-humanization, and I've only been that for four years. What is your condition?"

"That you look me in the eyes when you ask for what it is you need from me."

"That's it? Look you in the eyes?"

He nodded, his lips pursed, and I suddenly got very defensive. I remembered what it was like being his girlfriend, and why we broke up. The fights, the deceit, the lies. "Why do I need to look you in the eyes, Aldie? Because you think I might lie to you and—"

"No," he said with a force that stopped my would-be rant dead in its tracks. "Let us not follow that old script of distrust and anger. We might have once been monsters, but that was who they told us to be. The gods are gone, and they have taken their antiquated expectations of us with them. We must be different. We must change. And in changing, we will finally embrace the destiny that we chose, not the one chosen for us."

"Yeah, yeah … I get it. What's next? You're going to recommend I take a swim in Lake Me, or some bullshit like that?" I said, rolling my eyes. "I saw you out there. You seem to think that we're different because we're mortal now. Come on! It's not like you're not playing some game with them and getting paid through the nose to do so."

His stormy eyes grew grayer … not with sadness, but anger. "I am not that man anymore."

"Sure you aren't. Come on, it's just the two of us here. Fess up."

"I am not." He clenched his fist. Here came the Aldie I knew. Fiery and loud, ready to break the world with words that poisoned more than venom.

But instead of falling into a punishing rant, he took a deep breath before saying, "It is funny how the old demons struggle for renewed life. No matter how deep I bury him, he wants to take the reins again. But I will not allow that. Never again. I am mortal, and my 'new soul,' as you mock me for, demands that before the true me. A 'me' who will finally get a chance to embrace the full potential that was always nestled deep within."

"You should write a book." I picked up a copy of *The New Soul* sitting on his dresser. "Oh wait, you already did."

"Aye, milady, that I did."

↔

· · ·

"Kitty Kat," he started. "Sorry, Katrina. I am a different elf now. You may not believe that, but I am. I have embraced my destiny. And that destiny was to help Others."

"As in, with a capital O."

"No," he said, clearly listening in on my thoughts just like when we were together. "I mean it with a capital *Everyone*."

"Give me a self-help guru break, will you? Besides, since when did you get a destiny?"

"Since I searched my past and found it."

"So all the boozing, cheating, fighting and lying … it was hidden under there."

"No, it was hidden under the responsibility of my family that I once turned away from. They may have been the aristocrats of the UnSeelie Court, but they always wanted to help. That was their calling. And that was the calling they wanted for their wayward son. But they've been gone for a long time now, and so are the pressures I once hid behind. And it is in their absence that I pick up the mantle that was always my inheritance."

I wanted to roll my eyes, say something rotten and demeaning, but who was I to do so? I mean, I literally wore my father's mask from time to time. Was I also picking up his mantle?

As if answering a question I knew I hadn't spoken out loud, Aldie said, "It took me a while to understand them, and at first I didn't embrace all of my destiny, simply helping those before me. But their full manifestation requires that I be a role model for the world, not just a good person."

I thought about my father's Divine Cherubs, how he led them, guided them through the perils of the underworld. All I did was wear the mask and did what I thought was right when what was wrong presented itself to me. So no, I guess I hadn't fully picked up his mantle. Yet.

"So you've really changed?"

"I have."

"No more lying, fighting, cheating?"

"No more lying and cheating. I still throw down when needed." He lifted his fists up in the manner of a gentleman's fisticuffs.

"Alright, I believe you. And I need your help."

"Anything. Just—"

"Look you in the eyes. Got it." And so I did. I looked him in the eyes and told him everything.

When I was done, I felt like a great burden had been lightened. Not lifted off my shoulders, mind you, but lightened, like Aldie had volunteered to carry it with me.

"OK, my dear," he said. "I have a sure-fire plan to help your friends and get you to Paradise Lot. We can turn your friend back to a human through meditation."

"I doubt that listening to whale sounds and—"

"Trust me. The way I do it could turn a chicken into a scholar and a hyena into a boy. I'm extremely zen."

"I have no doubt you are."

"And as for getting back to Paradise Lot … I have a private jet. So, problem solved."

A private jet? Of course he did. But seeing as how he was going to help me and Deirdre and Egya get where we needed to go in that private jet, I only nodded. "Thank you, Aldie. I owe you one."

"Pish posh … you owe me nothing. Not after I—"

I lifted a silencing hand. "No. Not now. I'm being stalked by an ex-archangel. I don't think I can handle a heart-to-heart on top of all that."

"I understand. Another time. Until then, let us marvel at how destiny still works in this GoneGod World."

"Destiny?"

"Oh yes. I wasn't supposed to be in Japan until the start of the new year, but the vendors offered me the auditorium for free, as well as robust promotion. I may be rich, but I'm also a bargain hunter. I couldn't turn that down."

"Oh no." I grabbed his hand. "How could I be so stupid? Of course you'd be part of his plan."

"I don't understand."

"And you don't need to now. Now, we need to get out of here."

But before I could say another word, a raspy voice said, "What a wondrous reunion. I had planned on interrupting earlier, but I could not help myself. I wanted to see how far you two would go. I must thank you, Aldie. You have shown me the way to her heart."

"What? Who are—?" Aldie started, but before he could finish, Enoch held out a crystal-looking disk.

That was the last thing I saw before falling into total darkness.

↔

When I woke, Aldie and I were hanging from metal piping in some dank cellar. Our feet were several inches above the ground, and we were barefoot. *"Why do the assholes who are into creaky basements and torture always take off your shoes?"*

"To provide our guests with the most comfort," Enoch's voice rasped from behind us.

"Private thought," I shot back. "Not for you."

Enoch walked in front of me with what looked like one of those 18th century medical kits. "Oh, dear Kat. Very soon it will all be for me."

Aldie burst into speech. "The inner child always demands that the world give him everything, even when he has not earned it. But the path to true happi—"

Without turning around, Enoch pulled out four needles that were probably used to stitch up Frankenstein's monster and stabbed them into Aldie's chest.

"Ahh." Aldie let out a muted moan before catching his breath. "But the path to true happiness is purpose. And each one of our purposes is as unique as the fractal, crystalline patterns of a snowflake," he panted.

"Was he always like this?" Enoch asked with genuine curiosity.

"Oh yes," I said. "For as long as I've known him."

"Humph," Enoch said. "Torturing him will give me more satisfaction than I anticipated. But as for you, dear Kat, believe me when I say I will derive no pleasure from what comes next."

He punched me in the stomach.

"Well, I may have overstated my position. There will be a little pleasure in it for me."

To be continued ...

PART IV
INTERMISSION:

Metatron knows he should not meddle in the affairs of man, but to ask one such as him to do nothing now that he knows the gods are preparing to leave? Inconceivable. That is why he travels to Earth after hearing the Fates' words and seeing their tapestry.

He goes down to Earth to ... well ... meddle.

First he finds a creature of influence. A man of the cloth, as the humans say. This particular man is not only pious, but a human who possesses great resolve. Just like Metatron did when he, too, was mortal.

Tomás de Torquemada. A man capable of great love for God and little else. A man who will do anything and stop at nothing in the service of God.

Coming to this human as the angel that he is, he tells Tomás that humanity has lost its way. That their pitiful worship is not enough. He guides the human toward a great reformation, insisting that humans either fall to their knees in worship or death.

Imbuing this man with the tools necessary to usher in a new era, Metatron watches as the will of God is enforced on all. If such worship does not convince the gods to remain ...

Metatron does not allow himself to complete the thought. This will work.

This must work.

For the sake of all, the gods must remain.

↔

When the era the humans would later call the Grand Inquisition reaches its greatest heights, Metatron returns to the Fates to see how his influence has affected the future of all.

But the room housing the Fates' spindles, which created the Tapestry of Destiny, is not as he left it. Instead of the magnanimous weaver marching on and recording time yet to be, instead of every nanometer of fiber documenting a lifetime—every strand the rise and fall of an empire—the grand loom has ceased its endless chatter.

And at the fringes? Instead of the vibrant colors both named and unnamed, the last line ever woven is black. It's an ebony so deep that to gaze upon it is like staring into the very essence of nothing.

The three sisters slouch by their broken loom, none of them moving or speaking. A room that once held the wonders of the universe now feels like a back room in some war-torn bazaar.

Entering, Metatron feels something he has not felt since being transformed into an archangel.

Fear.

"What has happened here?"

"The loom no longer sees the future," the sisters chorus in despair.

"How can this be?"

Metatron does not know how the magics of destiny work. He doubts even the gods fully understand what the future is. What Metatron does understand is that the future is unset, can be molded by the hands of those working the present. It can always be changed. It can always be ... influenced.

But this darkness means that there is no future. There is nothing.

"Do the gods mean to destroy the universe?" Metatron mutters.

The eldest sister's shoulders slump even farther forward than before. She points to the corner in the back—the original patch she showed Metatron before. "Here is where the gods left. Here is the patch we showed you. But even with their departure, the loom wove a sea of black where the future could not be seen."

"Yes," says the second sister, "but now that you return, whatever it is you have done has ceased the weave."

The third echoes, "Whatever you have done has put this world on a path to nothing."

"What I have done?" Metatron's voice rises like a petulant child denying his actions. "I have forced the humans to believe again. I gave them the Inquisition. The movement will force them back to piety. Back to worship again."

"No, you have set the world on the path to its end."

Metatron does not believe it—cannot believe it. In his centuries of being the Watcher, Metatron has never lifted his hand in anger or violence. But in this moment he charges at the three sisters, subduing them under his power.

Then, as if plucking a ripe grape from its vine, he pulls out a single eye from each of the sisters. They scream in protest, but in his frenzy he does not hear them.

Using the infinite magic within him, he turns each of the eyes into lenses so that he may read the carpet's tapestry as they do.

He starts from the end, the blackness of nothing. He knows that the last weaves of the world do not speak of the end, for with every end there is a new beginning. The last weaves tell an anti-story where nothing will ever begin again.

This finality will occur after the gods depart. But how long after? He cannot tell.

Seeing that the end reveals nothing, he finds his own thread, examining it from the moment he first met the sisters.

He sees himself entering their chamber all those years ago. He relives the moment when they tell him about the gods' departure. He understands that they are trying to manipulate him into using his power to prevent the gods from leaving, and that they have succeeded.

He follows his actions, after which the carpet's weaving become erratic. Mottled.

Named and unnamed zigzags of colors play out. But instead of telling the story of all, they do so in chortled mutterings, like one trying to recall a dream. Fleeting and mottled.

But not all of the tapestry is confused. A few threads hold steady, marching forward through time with recognizable coherence. One of those threads intersects with his own.

Interlaced, it anchors his own destiny up to the point when the gods leave ... as if without it, his own future would be random and formless.

The two threads continue side by side. And side by side, they penetrate the moment when the gods leave.

Metatron leans in close, studying this thread with feverish vigor. "Who are you?" he mutters. In answer, his mind's eye presents a name. A human name that will guide his every action from this moment until long after the gods leave.

But at the moment of revelation, all Metatron can ask is, "Who is Katrina Darling?"

15

BEING TORTURED TO DEATH
WITH YOUR EX ISN'T FUN

"This is the part where the hero gets tortured. This is the scene where the villain comes up to the hero—moi—and waves some instrument of pain in her face, threatening this and that before finally stabbing her with the pointy bit. In the movies, the hero would resist and refuse to tell the villain anything (in this case, where the GoneGodDamn Soul Jar is). The villain will get frustrated, decide on another tack, buying the hero enough time for either a chance to escape, or for her friends to come in and save the day.

"Except I'm no hero. I'm just an ex-vampire trying to figure out what it means to be human again.

"I don't want to feel pain. I don't want to suffer. I just want to go home, snuggle up under my duvet and watch Legally Blonde. *So I should just tell him where the damn Soul Jar is and be done with it."*

I stared up from my precarious dangling position to where the villain and my ex-boyfriend stared at me in genuine bafflement.

"You were thinking out loud," Aldie finally said.

"Yeah, I do that."

Enoch, who had only moments earlier been edging toward me in that cliché menacing way, surgeon's scalpel in hand, stopped. He put down the blade and crossed his arms.

"Ahh," I said, "you were about to start torturing me."

"Indeed, but I think I'll take a moment to see how your thoughts pan out. If you take them to their only logical conclusion, I see a path which allows all this to be bypassed."

"You're still holding out hope?"

Enoch's eyes widened slightly, betraying that he did.

"After all this, you still think there is a chance for us."

"The Fates showed that you and I will be together in the end."

"Yeah, and they're never wrong?"

There was a slight creaking from the pipes that held Aldie. "Fates?"

"Apparently our torturer saw the two of us standing with the gods before the end of the world."

"Cool," Aldie said with genuine appreciation. "I get that."

"How the hell do you get that?" I growled, twisting just enough so that I could look into his stupid—perfect—dark elf face. "I just told you that this guy spoke to the Fates and that the last thing their damn visions showed him was him and me, together, in front of gods … *after* the world ends. And all you can say is, 'Cool … I get that,' like some damn stoned-out hippie tripping on laced weed."

"We all have a journey we must take, a destiny to fulfill."

"Are you shitting me now?" I yelled. "We're in a dank dungeon, suspended from the ceiling like curing meat, about to be tortured by a maniacal ex-archangel who, once he gets what he wants from us, is probably going to kill us. Well, *you* … I'm apparently supposed to be with him in the end. That said"—I gave Enoch my best disgusted look —"I think I'd prefer to die."

Aldie chuckled. "That's the Kat I know. Always using humor to hide her true feelings."

"Here's a true feeling for you: I want to kill you."

"No you don't. What you want is for me to stop speaking the truth."

"Oh my god! We're in serious shit and you're going all self-helpie on me. Tell me Mr. Guru, how exactly is that going to *self*-help us now?"

"Self-help isn't about the destination. It's about appreciating the journey. And right now, I appreciate that this man believes in what the Fates told him and is pursuing that goal with great enthusiasm."

"Ahhh! Please, please let me go so I can kill him. I swear I'll tie myself right back up."

Enoch chuckled before walking right over to Aldie and stabbing him in the gut.

So much for keeping up the banter.

↔

"What are you doing?" I yelled.

Enoch didn't say anything. He just stabbed Aldie again and again.

"Stop it!" I screamed, tears streaming down my face. "Stop it. You're killing him."

Enoch turned, lifting up his green, blood-stained hands. "What? I thought you wanted him dead?"

"No ... please stop." I looked at Aldie; he was bleeding out. He'd be gone in a few minutes if he didn't get help. "He's dying."

"And?"

"Save him. Please."

"Why should I?" Enoch wiped his hands on Aldie's shoulders—the only part of his clothes not covered in fae blood. "What will you do for me if I do?"

"What do you want?"

"You know."

"How can you expect us to be together after all the evil shit you've done?"

"Don't be coy with me," Enoch rasped. He took a deep breath to collect himself. "I have been thinking about us, and I have realized that, in my loneliness, I believed we would wind up together at the end of it all. But the Fates never showed our union. Just that we would be shoulder-to-shoulder when we next see the gods. I may have read more into that vision than was there." He pushed Aldie's body and it swung back and forth, drops of blood trickling on the floor. "Give me the Soul Jar, Katrina ... for his life."

"I can't."

"I promise you this: no one else need be hurt. The jar."

Aldie's almond skin was pale. He was dying. And as much as I hated him for everything he did to me, I couldn't let him die. I just couldn't.

"I gave it to Deirdre."

"Don't play me the fool. I saw what you handed to the changeling. It was but a trinket. The Soul Jar is much bigger. Certainly, larger than—"

"Gabriel ... he gave it to me in that form. He asked me to take it to Michael."

"Gabriel is dead."

"No ... I mean, yes. He's dead now, but he went to Yomi to retrieve it. He died to—"

"Of course," Enoch said, lost in thought. "The angel knew my soul had been trapped in that damn thing. He knew of the dead gods, but there is more at play here. Why not leave the jar in the museum?"

"I don't know. He just said I was to take it to Michael."

"Those damn archangels are trying to find their way to the gods. They must be."

"Enoch ... Aldie. Help him!"

The force of my voice woke Enoch from his musing. "What? Oh yes ..." The ex-archangel walked over to Aldie, pulled out a handkerchief from his pocket and placed it over his wound. Instantly the bleeding stopped, and the wound healed.

Aldie hung silent for an impossibly long moment before he coughed. "That was ... something else."

"The Veil of Veronica, used to wipe the blood and sweat from Jesus. It offered him comfort during his greatest struggle. Now it offers healing to all of us." Enoch said, pulling out a cell phone from his pocket. "Now if you'll excuse me, I have a necklace to retrieve."

"Let him go," I said.

"Most certainly not. I need him hanging right there so that I can stab him again should your words prove false."

With that, Enoch stepped out of the dimly lit room to call whatever manner of horror served as his minion.

And what did Aldie have to say for his near-death experience?

"Well, this is interesting."

16

MEMORIES, SWINGING DEATH
AND GROWLING KATS

*I*t's amazing how three simple words and a bit of torture can take you right back to where you were with someone you haven't seen in centuries. I remembered back to the decade before we separated, what had happened to him and how he reacted then.

We were engaged, about to be married. Of course, fae engagements tended to last centuries, and wedding preparations alone took upward of *years*. Had we stayed together, our wedding would have been in June … fifty-seven years from now.

Not that I cared back then. I was in love, and whether we married didn't really matter to me. So we prepared, hiring cake makers and a wedding dressmaker, caterers and the premier florist in all of the UnSeelie Court. But with the fae, hiring someone like that meant arranging the wedding around their schedule. Which meant waiting a long, long time. Like I said: fifty-seven years from today.

What's more, because the flower arrangement was more important than the dress, not only did it mean waiting for the florist's schedule to free up, it also meant waiting for the florist to grow the damn flowers … And because Aldie's parents were revered, the florist insisted on developing a new strain of orchid just for the occasion. We broke up before the flower was grown, but its petals were to be blood red to represent the human (and vampire) in me, with veins of deep, forest green for Aldie's fae heritage.

But the fae were still trying to accept that the last son to be born into the fae courts was marrying an outsider—and a half-breed to boot—so waiting centuries also meant enduring the underhanded comments, snide remarks and passive aggression against us.

Everyone seemed to hate me, and hate our union even more (maybe that's why I empathize with Others so well; I know what it's like to be rejected just because you're different) ... everyone but Aldie's parents.

They were the kindest fae you'd ever meet, and even though they were dark fae skilled in espionage and sabotage, they never treated me with anything but kindness.

And they were celebrated of sorts, both of them highly respected academics who were directly credited for ending the war with the Seelie Court.

They loved me. Every time they looked at me, their huge elven eyes would soften. There was no pity there; they knew full well what the other fae were like toward me, and they knew I was tough enough to handle it, too.

No, they loved me for reasons I never quite understood, immediately accepting me into their family.

Then they were killed. Poisoned with venom extracted from the Thistle of Salt, a highly deadly substance aptly named because nothing can grow once salted, and for fae, to *not* grow was to die.

Ultimately it was uncovered that a faction among the UnSeelie Court, resentful over how Aldie's parents' had ended the war, had come after them. Of course, that wasn't until I was blamed, Aldie was blamed and the entire Seelie Court was blamed. But that is, perhaps, a story for another time.

The reason why all those horrible memories flooded back to me was because Aldie said those same words with the same detached tone when we discovered his parents' bodies. *"This is interesting."*

"You're not fooling anybody," I said.

"Excuse me?"

"This is interesting," I repeated.

"Oh," he said, and I knew that he, too, remembered that moment. "Well, it is. My parents always taught me to soak in every experience and learn what I can from it. I've learned a lot in these last moments."

"And what exactly have you learned?" I meant it rhetorically. I wasn't really waiting for an answer; instead, I was trying to find a way out of here. The binds that Enoch used on us were solid, and the pipes were firmly fixed to the ceiling. There was just enough space above the piping for someone my size to crawl along, if I could swing high enough. I tried, but quickly learned that there was no way I would be able to gather enough momentum to loop all the way around.

At a loss as to what to try next, I twisted to look at Aldie. I recognized the outline of Light-Bringer in his pants' pocket—that old gift from his parents so many centuries ago. Of course he still kept it … even if it was just a lighter. It was from *them*. But besides holding it up to the sprinklers and hoping Enoch would melt, the lighter wouldn't do us any good right now.

Aldie wore a pensive look on him, and I realized he was still considering my question—as rhetorical as it was. "All of it," he eventually said.

"All of what?" I said, rolling my eyes.

"This," he said with a voice full of vigor and optimism as he held my gaze with elven eyes that burned with intensity. "All of this. Think about what an amazing opportunity we have to learn about ourselves. How many people are truly tested in such a manner? How many are given such a golden opportunity to learn about themselves in this way?"

"And what have you learned about yourself, exactly?" This time I wasn't being rhetorical—I really wanted to know, because I didn't imagine he'd come up with anything good.

I groaned, pulling myself up. Maybe if I could swing my feet up, I'd be able to get up there. It was no use. Human bodies simply weren't designed to contort that way.

"I've learned that I don't like being tortured."

"You needed to be stabbed to learn that?" If my hands were free, I'd be pinching the bridge of my nose in frustration. Instead I settled for major eye-rollings—as in, plural. Not that he noticed any of it. As callous as this was, I prayed that Aldie was experiencing some form of post-traumatic stress disorder, because I couldn't come up with another explanation for his behavior right now.

Aldie rocked his hips lightly from side to side, causing his body to casually sway back and forth. If I didn't know him better, I'd assume he was trying to escape. But I did know him better. He wasn't trying to escape—he was enjoying the hanging sensation. He was also humming. I hated it when he hummed back when we were together. I hated it even more now that we weren't.

"What are you doing now?" I asked in that same rhetorical tone which, if he were a normal creature, he would have understood. But Aldie, being Aldie, answered everything.

"Processing," he mused. "I've learned that I don't like being stabbed."

"I could have told you that without you actually being stabbed. Could have saved you a lot of pain."

"Pain is only unworthy when we do not learn from it."

"And the pain of this conversation is teaching me how much of a pain in the ass you are."

"Ahh, my dear little sphinx, how little you have changed. You still confuse temporary discomfort with actual pain. You have never stopped to consider what is it that truly hurts you, and because you are unaware of that, you do not know what your true purpose is. The day my parents died was the day I was set on the path toward my true purpose. Perhaps this day will set you on yours." Aldie was far too calm for someone who had just been brought back from the dead for the explicit purpose of being killed again.

His calmness was utterly infuriating. "Right now, my true purpose is to get free so I can punch you in the nose. I hate to ask, but can you burn a wee bit of time and get us out of here?"

Aldie shook his head. "This torturer of yours is somehow stopping me from using my magic."

"Sounds like Enoch. He has a magical item for everything."

115

"You speak as if you admire him."

I pursed my lips, annoyed that he was listening in on my thoughts.

Aldie didn't notice. "And as to your earlier comment, I believe that one's true purpose is to live to their fullest potential while honoring who they were meant to be. Punching me in the nose is only a part of that."

I screamed. This time, it wasn't from Enoch's physical torture, but from the mental torture of being with this dark elf.

"Yes," Aldie said, unshaken by my cries. "My little cat is finally embracing her lion's roar."

He lifted his knees up, gathering himself in a fetal position. That's when I first noticed he still wore that weird gray, plastic chip around his neck. A trinket or something … I couldn't quite make out what it was from where I hung. But whatever it was, he deemed it important enough to try to grab with his knees.

He managed to clasp it between his knees, and lifting them up to his mouth, he bit down hard on the plastic tile. Then he let himself hang again, dropping the tile on the ground.

"What are you doing?"

"Trying to—"

Enoch entered with a giant grin on his face. "Seems that Katrina does care for you, dark elf. Her words were true. The Soul Jar is being retrieved now."

I thought about how my cowardice had put Egya and Deirdre in danger and hoped the two of them were smart enough to hand it over without getting hurt.

"Let him go," I said.

"No," Enoch rasped. "He stays until the jar is in my possession."

"Then what?"

Enoch's silence told me exactly what he planned to do.

17

VILLAINS WILL ALWAYS BE VILLAINS

"*Awkward silences are awkward in the best of circumstances, but when they're between you and your torturer, well, let's just say that it takes awkward to a whole new level.*

"*But here we are, two hanging torturees and a torturer with nothing to say between us. What do you break the silence with? A joke? Some weird factoid about how golf balls were created and why they have dimples? Interesting story—*"

"Will you please shut up?" Enoch said.

"What? My nervous ramblings are bothering you? Tell you what … why not cut me down and I'll take my inner thoughts elsewhere."

Enoch gave me a look that I'm certain once brought demigods to their knees. Since I was hanging, kneeling wasn't an option. "You can give me your cold 'I'm Judge, Jury and Executioner' look all you want. As the torturee in this fucked-up relationship, I get to express myself, whether it be screaming and crying, or my inner thoughts babbling away."

"I wouldn't call it babbling," Aldie chuckled. He had passed out for a bit—I guess dying and being brought back takes it out of you—and I wasn't sure how long he'd be out. "I am really curious as to why golf balls have dimples."

"Well—"

"Enough," Enoch rasped. Then coughed. I figured that once upon a time, he used to boom his commands with a voice that was deep and resonant. But given how messed up his throat was, he couldn't really do that anymore, and the effort irritated his throat to the point of near choking.

"Would you like me to get you some water?" I imbued my tone with as much insincere sympathy as I could.

Aldie chuckled. "Ahh, I remember why I loved you so."

"Do you?" I twisted my dangling body so I could see him. "And do you remember why you left me?"

Aldie winced, before nodding. "I do."

"And ..."

"And?"

"And you left me because ..." I let the last word hang in much the same fashion as I was.

"Do you really want to discuss our end while we hang on for dear life?"

"I do." And I really did. Normally this kind of banter would be me probing for an exit. You know, the old fake a fight, distract our captor, get out of here. But as I said those words, I was struck by how much I really did want to know and how little I was trying to find an escape at that very moment.

"Katrina, now is not the time."

"And when exactly would the time be? We're probably going to die here. Well, you're probably going to die. Me—this weirdo seems to think we will be married one day. So if not now, when?"

"Hold on, he wants to marry you?"

"Desire and destiny are two different things," Enoch rasped. He was dabbing his lips with a handkerchief and I saw blood stains on the cloth. Somehow, I didn't think that blood was because he opened up an old wound. He was coughing blood and, in my experience, when you did that it was because you were sick. As in, dying-sick.

"I once thought I also desired her hand," Enoch continued. "But after getting to know her better, I came to realize that a true union is not possible. She is the proverbial stallion that cannot be tamed."

"Amen to that," Aldie said.

"Amen to that?" I groaned. "First of all, Aldie, you are fae. Fae don't amen anything. Secondly, are you really agreeing with the guy who just stabbed you?"

"I am."

"Because?"

"Because he speaks the truth, and the ugliness of our current circumstances does not exempt me from hearing and agreeing with it." Aldie spoke in the same tone he used when making one of his self-help, holier-than-thou points.

"Screw you."

"Interesting fact about that term. Much like the golf ball, it too comes from Scotland. Scottish prisons, to be accurate. In the 1800s, prison guards would—"

"Shut up," Enoch and I said in unison.

Aldie chuckled before another heavy silence came over us.

We must have hung like that for a couple minutes before the dark elf sighed. "If I am to live by my principles, then I must die by them, too."

"What's that supposed to mean?"

"When the gods left, they shattered one of the oldest lies they ever told—that they would be there for us always."

"I don't know about that," I said.

"You are human. Your god never walked amongst your kind."

"Except once," Enoch corrected.

"Except once," Aldie agreed. "But even then, he did so in such an ambiguous moment and during a time of unreliable records. It is difficult for a modern human to believe. But we fae, our gods were amongst us. Dined with us. Mated with us. They continuously reminded us that they would care for us. And then they left without so much as a word as to why or guidance as to what we were to do next. So, you see—a lie.

"I vowed to never lie again. Not speaking, especially with the uncertainty of ever receiving another chance, is a lie by omission. And since the chances of us ever speaking again are negligible, allow me to answer your question. I left because you wanted me to."

"Excuse me?" This time I twisted my body completely around so I could give him my own death stare. But since I was hanging in the way I was, all I managed to do was twist around and give him a split-second death stare before turning around again.

So, I twisted again. And again.

Twist, death stare, turn. Twist, death stare, turn.

"I was a young vampire—only eighty years or so. I was alone, without a sire to guide me or a coven to protect me. You were my world. I loved you. I loved living in the UnSeelie Court. I loved your parents."

"I know," Aldie said. "And they loved you, too. But none of that was enough for us to remain together. You wanted something else."

"And what was that?"

"You wanted what we all do: to find your purpose. And even though you couldn't articulate it then, deep down you knew that your purpose was not with me. It was the hardest thing I ever did, letting you go. But it was also the right thing to do."

"You turned me away. Right after your parents ..." I stopped talking.

"Died," Aldie finished for me. "I will forever be in your debt for what you did for me."

"What she did?" Enoch lifted a curious eyebrow.

"What, your celestial stalking of me didn't mention that? The Fates' tapestry didn't show you what happened then?" I growled. "Aldie's parents were something of celebrities in the UnSeelie Court, so when they died, the court employed all manner of detectives and magic to find their killers. And who did they wind up pointing their slender, perfectly formed elven fingers at? Aldie. He was going to be executed, but I was on the case. I found his parents' killers and brought them to justice. And what did Aldie do as thanks for giving his parents peace and saving his ass? He kicked me to the curb."

"I set you free."

"You can use all the flowery language you want—you dumped me. Coldly and harshly."

"Katrina," Aldie said in that tone he used when he was trying to cut through my anger to get me to listen, "I saw who you were when you were—how did you put it? On the case? You were alive. Not the sullen girl you became when you joined me at the elven theater or dinner parties, wearing fae silks and perfume. Being the half-breed demon of a dark elf aristocrat muted you. And I couldn't do that anymore. Not after seeing your vibrant colors during my own darkest days. I loved you far too much for that."

I thought back to that moment. He was right. I was so ... engaged when I was trying to save Aldie. But I didn't just do it for him. His parents had been kind to me. I loved them. I *needed* to see their true killers brought to justice.

But it was more than that. Finding his parents' killers in the unfriendly world of the fae was a real challenge, and I loved every minute of it.

There was a slow clap from the corner. "I must applaud that little display, and thank you, dear dark elf, for unveiling more about Katrina to me. I now see that our union will never be. Still, the Fates showed us hand in hand, standing before the gods. That image was clear, and the Fates are never wrong."

Aldie cracked his neck. "The Fates are also never clear. They play their old parlor tricks of obfuscation and sleight of hand, using words with double meanings. You saw your union because that's what you wanted to see. You saw the two of you standing before the gods because, again, that's what you wanted to see. But the truth is, the gods are gone. Whoever you were standing before is not the gods. It is just the false glamor of an old—"

"NO," Enoch growled. "I saw it clear. She and I were standing hand in hand on the shores of some great ocean. Five gods from different pantheons stood before us, all of them looking down on us with smiles on their faces. Behind them, the sun was dipping below the horizon."

"Where?"

"Wherever they are now."

"Tell me, Enoch, why would the gods be standing on a beach at sunset? Because they are marrying you two?"

"I do not presume. But that is the location where we met them."

"And why would they be smiling?"

"They are pleased that we found them."

"Remember," I said, "he wants to destroy the world and go on some supernova cosmic ride to find them."

"Answer me this, Enoch. After everything you have seen of this woman, do you still believe that she will join your little voyage? Don't you think it is more likely that she will die before that?"

Enoch didn't say anything. And neither did I. I did, however, let Aldie's words sink in. If he was right, then I would never leave this planet.

Still, what if what Enoch saw was also right? Were the gods planning to come back? And if they did, what would become of this world? We barely survived their leaving, and I knew we had no chance of surviving their return.

But before I could fully consider the implications of those thoughts, Enoch started laughing with those eerie, raspy croaks of his. "Very clever, dark elf. Oh, how your lies do distract."

"I am not lying. I told you that I do not lie. Not anymore."

"Really?" Enoch said. "You mentioned that the Fates used obfuscation and sleight of hand to fool those who would listen. Tell me, how are you different?"

"Because I do not manipulate. I am not trying to get my audience to do or believe something that is false. I am merely trying to inspire."

"Inspire through lies."

"No," Aldie said, but I could hear his voice wobble.

"And those little pyrotechnics, those fireballs. Tell me, how much time do you burn for each?"

Aldie didn't answer.

"Wait a minute," I said. "Are you telling me that those fireballs were an illusion? As in a non-magical, I'm-a-Vegas-magician illusion?"

Again, my question was met with silence.

"Aldie," I said.

The dark elf let out a long sigh. "Pockets of gas released, then ignited in midair. Ingenious, don't you think?"

"So, you weren't sacrificing time?"

"That's not entirely true. It took time to design that. And also, I needed to burn a bit of magic to explode the gas—"

"How much?"

Enoch smiled at my question. He was loving this.

Even though I couldn't see him, I knew him well enough to know that he lifted an eyebrow in a very Spock-like fashion. "How much what?"

"How much time?"

"It took me several tries and singeing my hair twice, so all invested, a week?"

I shook my head. "Don't play coy with me. How much?"

"Three seconds."

"You burnt three seconds of time per fireball?" I didn't know if I wanted to punch him or scream.

"No, three seconds total."

OK, I did know. I wanted to scream *and* punch him.

"You lied."

"They needed a hero," he said. "Someone to sacrifice for them. Like their gods once did. That is all I did."

"You lied," I repeated.

"No! I inspired."

"And now you're lying to yourself."

"They needed a hero."

"A false god," Enoch rasped.

"Oh, don't give me that shit," I said, locking eyes with Enoch. "Your god was just as false as him. And a worse hero, too."

"Excuse me?" Enoch's eyes widened.

"God makes a terrible hero," I said. "Think about it, when you can do anything with simply a thought, there is no struggle. No overcoming anything."

"You ungrateful talking monkey—" He took a step toward me.

"You're a talking monkey, too. And criticize him as much as you want," I said. "Your hero is just as bad."

"Maybe you are right," Enoch rasped. "Maybe you foolish humans didn't want a god. You wanted a hero to believe in, not a god to worship. You wanted Him to believe in you. And when He rightly refused, you stopped worshipping Him. You took Him for granted. You turned your back on Him first. You ..." He punched a hard, accusing finger against my chest, causing me to swing under the force of each painful *"you."*

"You," he said one more time. He gave us his back, not wanting me to see the glossy tears of frustration welling up.

He was hurting, and if he wasn't hell-bent on torturing me before destroying all life, I might have felt sorry for him.

I will give it to Enoch. Of all the villains (*moi* included) I've known over my long, long life, he was the most methodical—the deadliest of all. And that included the three dead gods I had the displeasure of meeting. But when you boiled it all down, he was still just a villain. And villains seem to all share the same trait of getting emotional.

Probably comes from their moms not hugging them enough. I know that was my excuse.

And when they get emotional, they make mistakes.

The force of Enoch's finger on my chest caused me to swing more and more each time he prodded me. Pretty soon, my body was moving back and forth like a pendulum. I kicked back my foot to increase my momentum as I swung back, and as soon as I swung forward, I used Enoch's chest as a springboard to twist round and up over the pipe.

I had seconds until Enoch would find a way to reach me, but seconds were all I needed. Shimmying the ropes along the pipe, I moved toward the bolt that held the section of pipe on which we hung.

I may not weigh much, but old pipes like this weren't designed to hold much of anything. Laying on my back, I kicked up against the wall and pushed with all my worth.

The joints creaked, then groaned before finally giving way. With a rush of water, the pipes cracked apart and, although still bound, I was free.

And so was Aldie.

With the grace of a mountain lion, he flipped forward, kicking Enoch's chest. The blow forced the ex-archangel a few steps back, buying us enough time to make it out of the room, where a conveniently hung sign with the word *Exit* on it pointed the way.

18

ANGELS AND ELVES ... LET'S GET READY TO RUMBLE!

*E*noch hadn't taken us far. We were in the bowels of the auditorium. Makes sense—he would have needed to sneak us past thousands of adoring fans ... *non*-human fans who tend to have extra eyes and boundary issues. Who knows how many satyrs, pixies and elves had burnt a few minutes of time to sneak into his dressing room? Aldie was friggin' hot!

Even though we were literally running for our lives, that last thought filled me with a pang of jealousy. How many groupies did he grope? *Oh groan, Kat. You really need to work on your phrasing.*

No time to think about that now. We needed to get upstairs and away. Enoch burst out of the room, clutching his chest. Whatever Aldie did took him by surprise, and the one thing I was starting to figure out about Enoch was that he was only uber-powerful when he was prepared. Catch him off guard and he was as fragile as any human.

As Enoch moved, he fumbled with one hand as he put something in his ear. What was it? Another magical device that gave him ... what? ESP? Telekinetic powers? Spidey-senses?

I glanced back as we started up the stairs and saw that Enoch was mumbling something. A neon-blue light emanated from whatever was in his ear as he spoke. *"Hold on,"* I thought. *"that's not a magical item —that's an earpiece for his ph—"*

It's times like this I need to think faster. The door at the top of the stairs burst open, and the biggest friggin' angel I'd ever seen opened the door.

Oh joy.

↔

Throughout the ages, human mythology has told stories about vast receptacles of knowledge. The Library of Alexandria, the Temple of Apollo and others … all places that housed unfathomable wisdom. And in every instance, there was always an accompanying legend that saw to its destruction. The Library of Alexandria burned down. Apollo abandoned and ravaged by time.

So when the internet was being developed, the human in me went, "Oh yes, finally myth becomes reality." The demon in me said, "Whatever … the humans are going to muck this one up, too."

I always thought my inner demon was right. After all, the internet seemed to be used exclusively for porn, memes and musing over stupid things, like: Who would win in a fight—a crocodile or a shark?

What was the appeal?

But seeing Aldie face off against that massive, hulking angel, I suddenly wished the internet had asked: Who would win in a fight—a dark elf or an angel?

The angel growled, his huge frame literally bulking up as he tensed his muscles. Normally angels are beautiful, even the ones created for war. But this guy had patches of hair missing from burns that never healed, and his left eye was glossed over—a dead, useless sphere that only remained by the grace of the muscles holding it there.

Not that being blind in one eye stopped him from seeing us.

Without any of the preamble typical of a villain's henchman, he slammed his fist down toward us.

Aldie, faster than I'd thought, pushed me to one side as he pivoted to the other. He was fast, graceful ... unbelievably fluid. He even managed to quip, "What? No foreplay?" as he did so. I immediately saw Aldie's tactic: he was trying to get behind the angel.

But fighting an angel isn't just dodging fists and feet. They fought dirty. They used their wings.

The angel spread his wings, creating shutters that extended to the two sides of the hall. There was no getting behind him from the sides, but as big as angel wings were, they still only had two feet. I dove in between his legs and kicked the back of his knee.

I don't care how big you are—kick there and you're going down. The angel went down to one knee like he was proposing to Aldie, who promptly responded by putting a hand on his shoulder and a foot on his chest. He was looking to flip over him.

And just as he was about to do it, the angel shot up both of his wings, catching Aldie's chin and sending him flying back toward Enoch.

"Run," Aldie said as he got to his feet. "I'll take care of these two scoundrels." The dark elf stood in the classic gentleman boxer's pose from the 1800s. Pretty, but not a very effective fighting stance.

Aldie knew he didn't have a chance against one of them, let alone two. And ever the showman, if he was going down he'd make it a grand exit, even if there wasn't anyone to see it.

Aldie was screwed. But I wasn't. I was behind the angel, and the only thing that stood between me and the exit was my own sense of right and wrong.

I tried to will my feet to move. To get out of here. To leave Aldie to the fate before him. The GoneGods knew he deserved it, after the way he left me. But seeing that elf standing there, ready to sacrifice all for a cause that he'd only heard about just hours earlier, and knowing what he did for the Others ... Sure, there were lots of parlor tricks going on and he was misleading them, but his heart was in the right place. I couldn't leave him.

But what could I do against these two, even if I was behind them? Well, the only thing one can do in such a situation. I fought the fire of their hate with a fire of my own.

A real one.

↔

The outer feathers of an angel's wings are made of some celestial, impossibly hard material not dissimilar from Teflon (if Teflon were as light as, well … a feather, and capable of repelling a missile). Those super-powerful things were impervious to fire, acid, ice and oil. Which means throwing one of those otherwise devastating substances at an angel is useless. But what few people know is that's just what the *outer* feathers can do.

The inner layers are made of the exact same feathers as geese, making an angel-feather duvet just an expensive gimmick. It also means that angel wings are highly flammable. "Aldie—Light-Bringer, throw it to me," I yelled.

I don't know if the dark elf knew what my plan was, but he threw me his lighter without hesitation. Despite the giant angel between us, it was a perfect throw. Then Aldie did something I didn't expect. He charged at the angel seeking to … what? Wrestle with him?

Dark elves are strong, but they're nothing compared to an angel bred for battle. So if Aldie was to win against this creature, he needed to use his agility. But he didn't do that at all.

The angel got down on all fours and met Aldie's charge full on. The two struck each other with such tremendous force that I felt the shockwaves. The two powerful beings were locked in a wrestling match to the death. Aldie held his own, but I could see his muscles straining. It was only a matter of time before the angel overpowered him.

He would lose. And despite that, he wore a smile. So did Enoch, who stood by the door, watching. But despite Enoch's grin, he clutched his chest, standing perfectly still like one trying to conserve his energy.

Why did he need to? He was about to have the Soul Jar, and he had Aldie trapped. And with all those magical items at his disposal, he could hunt me down at his leisure ... if I was still a concern to him. I suspected I was enough of a pain that he'd probably be cutting his *We were meant to be* losses on the marrying Kat front.

I looked at Light-Bringer in my hand, its weight immense for what I needed from it now. I struck its archaic flint, praying to gods who would not listen that the old thing struck true.

Nothing.

I struck again.

Nothing.

But on the third attempt, the orange flame of non-magical fire sprouted to life. I jumped on the angel's back and wiggled my hands in between the angel's wings, down into the inner layers where I found some nice, normal, non-magical feathers that caught fire without protest.

Immediately, black smoke came billowing out of the angel's back.

The angel didn't seem to notice. I knew he was locked in a test of strength against Aldie, but angels are acutely aware of their bodies. He knew he was on fire ... and he didn't care.

So I punched him square in his left temple. That should get his attention. Nothing. If the angel felt it, he made no sign of it. The billowing smoke grew. More and more of the angel's feathers were catching fire.

"Oche." Enoch coughed at the effort of saying the angel's name. "Oche ... please."

In his embrace with Aldie, I heard the angel utter between strained breaths, "I almost have him."

"Oche, please. They are of little concern. Take care of yourself before something happens to your wings that cannot be repaired."

"But Enoch," Oche said.

"I can bear much," Enoch rasped. "But I cannot bear real harm coming to a beautiful angel such as you. Please."

Oche stopped fighting Aldie and, standing erect, slammed his back against the wall, patting out the fire.

Aldie didn't need to be told twice. Panting from his fight, he ran past the angel, and taking my hand, we made our way to the exit.

↔

On the other side of the door, I saw we had made our way backstage. "We need to find Deirdre and Egya."

"Egya?"

"The hyena."

"Ahh yes, the shapeshifter who can't shift back."

"And then we need to regroup and find those two. They have the Soul Jar and—"

Aldie produced a tiny, unassuming jar that hung from an equally innocuous chain. "Is this it?"

I grabbed it out of his hand. "How did you—?"

"During my fight with that horrific angel. He had it on him and, well, a good pickpocket knows he must get close."

"But how did you know I would stop him?"

"Because a good pickpocket also knows when to trust their partner in crime." He squeezed my hand as he said the word *partner*.

A squeeze that sent familiar desire coursing through me.

I shook my head. Thoughts of him ... of us ... would have to wait.

"We have the jar," I said, pulling my hand away so I could think straight, if nothing else. "They'll be after us now. We need to get out of here. We need to find a way to Paradise Lot."

PART V
INTERMISSION:

Metatron has learned from the Fates that today is the day the gods will leave. And so he prepares, laying out everything he needs. It has been so long since he was human that he can't quite remember what it takes to kill one. Fire, slitting the throat. Hanging.

Such methods take time. Seems the human body is loath to shake off its mortal coil, and he needs his death to be instant.

The methods he has before him would take far too long. By his estimation, he has exactly three minutes to die.

That is, once he becomes human again.

Three minutes. One hundred and eighty seconds. An eternity.

He truly wishes he had a bomb or a gun. Such instruments of destruction would grant him the instant death he needs.

But alas, such instruments of destruction are forbidden in Heaven. And that is exactly where he needs to die. In Heaven, and in the moments before the gods leave.

So Metatron decides to hedge his bets by using several tools at once. Placing a rope around his neck, he pulls it taut, allowing himself to hang. In his present form, he feels nothing. He is just hanging from a rope.

But as soon as he becomes human again, as soon as his divinity leaves him ... Well then, the rope will cut off his oxygen, and that is how humans die. Lack of oxygen.

"Seems like a design flaw," he muses.

Next, he lifts the blade to his neck. He plans to plunge it deep into his—what did the angel Penemue call it?—aortic vein. Once his heart resumes beating, it will pump out the red blood that will start to flow in his body again.

That should speed up the process.

But it still might not be fast enough, so Metatron plans to also plunge the blade into his belly and cut out his guts in the fashion performed by so many Japanese warriors. He understands this method to be final and brutal. And fast.

That's what he needs: fast.

Death should be easier than this, but also, after being an immortal angel for all this time, he has lost touch with what it means to be alive.

Or human.

Metatron hangs in the ready, taking a moment to look out the window of his chamber. He knows that the all-consuming darkness will come from the east, the direction his window faces.

Then, looking at his former study, he smiles as he observes the chest of celestial treasures. He is, after all, its guardian. Within that simple box countless artifacts reside, many given to him by the gods as thanks for his numerous deeds. It is said there is no treasure more valuable that what that chest contains, and Metatron wonders if his soul will be able to pick up the chest so that he may take it with him.

Chuckling to himself, he remembers an old human adage: You can't take it with you. He suspects those words are true.

Still, he'll try. No point in leaving behind an immortal lifetime of accomplishments.

As his mind contemplates such things, the fated words he was waiting for—the ones that have played in his head over and over again —finally ring out: "Thank you for believing in us, but it is not enough. We're leaving. Good luck."

When will it come?

As if in answer to his question, a mighty horn sounds.

In an instant, Metatron becomes human again.

The archangel Metatron has reverted back to the mortal once known as Enoch.

↔

Metatron, or rather Enoch, had forgotten what being human is like. For one thing, human bodies are frail, weak. Soft.

For another, the pain these bodies are capable of feeling is incredible. More design flaws.

As soon as his body regains its mortality, the rope bites into his neck, pulling taut and cutting off the oxygen that he forgot how desperately the human body needs.

Instead of stabbing himself in the neck and then carving out his guts, Enoch drops his dagger to the ground as both his hands grab at the rope.

He is trying to get free. He wants to be loose, to breathe again.

No, that's not right. The thought finds its way through the hurricane of panic his mind suffers from. He doesn't want to be free. He doesn't want to breathe again. He wants to die.

Death is the only way the human soul will leave its body. And the human soul is the only creation that can follow the gods.

He sees the rolling darkness through his window. It approaches far too quickly. He doubts that death will come soon enough for him to follow. Not without a dagger hastening his demise.

They will be gone, and so will he. But his departure will be the finality of nothing.

He'd laugh at the cruelty of it all, if only the rope would let him.

The world begins to blink out as his eyes close, giving into what is soon to come. Death. Nothing. No more.

But death does not come. Instead, he feels powerful arms lift him up as a talon snaps the rope.

He is placed on the ground and a soft, familiar voice asks, "Metatron, what are you doing? What is happening?"

An angel, but one who had no idea of the gods' plans. She—or is it a he?—must have come here after the gods' message, seeking Metatron's wisdom.

The angel's face is blurred, and he cannot quite make out who it is … But despite his weakened condition, he can feel the angel's panic.

Still by his side, the angel is no longer looking at him, her attention on the window. "By the power of Heaven, what is that darkness? It is consuming everything."

"The end," Enoch tries to say. His voice comes out harsh. Broken. "The end," he rasps again. "It has come to consume us. We must leave or die."

Without hesitation, the angel picks up Enoch's frail, mortal body. "Wait," he rasps, his hand reaching out to his artifacts.

But he is too weak to say or do more. Instead, merciful unconsciousness takes him. As he drifts away, he has two thoughts that are ironically at odds.

The first is a prayer that he will never wake.

The second is a hope. He hopes he does wake … so that he may dedicate his life to finding a way back to his God.

19

REGROUPING THE BREAKOUT GROUPS

*W*e made our way to the upper levels. Enoch and his giant minion, Oche, wouldn't be far behind. As we ran, I kept expecting a huge, talon-filled hand to grab me. Getting out of the basement was high on my priority list.

Until, that was, we actually did find the closest exit and managed to get to the main floor. The massive conference hall was empty.

"Where is everyone?" Aldie asked. "What time is it?"

"I don't know," I said. "But we've been below for hours. It's the middle of the night. You can't expect any of your groupies to still be hanging around and—"

A bell rang, and the conference doors opened. Others of all walks of life spilled out into the hall. "What the—?"

"Breakout groups," Aldie said. "We run hard for three days. No breaks. No sleep. Just a relentless drilling down on the problems of mortality."

"You've got to be kidding me," I said as a swarm of Others ran toward Aldie.

↔

. . .

Aldie was immediately overrun by adoring fans who didn't seem to notice that his clothes were stained with green blood. Nor the slash marks on his shirt where Enoch had stabbed him. I guess we see what we need to see, and right now, as they wrestled with their own issues of mortality, the last thing they needed to see was their hero dying.

Just like they didn't need to know about the tricks he used with the fireballs.

What they wanted was hope. And Aldie, for all that he'd just gone through, delivered that in spades. At first I thought there was no hope for us to get through the crowd. They were all around. But Aldie was a pro. He simply raised his hand and said in a commanding but soft voice, "Fellow Others, hear me now."

Immediately the crowd went silent. Aldie reverted to his normal voice. "Clear a path so that I may lead you to the next, unscheduled event."

The Others standing in front of him stepped aside, giving Aldie and me space to move through.

I couldn't help but stare at Aldie with admiration. He was better than the Pied Piper. "In life—in *mortal* life—we must always be ready to accept the deviations presented to us. We must always be ready to follow new paths, new directions. That is why I am changing tonight's activities. Follow me."

"Is the breakout session on 'Food: Which Dead Creatures Are Socially Acceptable to Eat' cancelled?" asked a despondent ghoul.

"I'm afraid so."

"Ooh, but it's all so confusing."

"Such is life. But don't worry, we'll email you the PDF guide," Aldie said with a wink.

"Are humans on the list?"

"I'm afraid not."

"What are you doing?" I whispered to Aldie.

"Getting us out of here. Those maniacs aren't going to attack us in this crowd. And even if they did, they'd have to face off against all of them." He turned with those last words so that he was walking backward. "Tell me, what is the harshest thing about being mortal?"

"Headaches," a three-headed cerberus said. "I get them in all my heads at once. Can't burn time to make them go away. Must consume something called Tylenol."

"Bowel movements," a raijin said. "Never had those before."

"When can you trample your neighbor to death and when can you not?" brayed a centaur.

"Never," I said to the centaur. "The answer is never."

The centaur stomped his hind leg. "So unfair."

"There are so many rules. Then, all of sudden, there don't seem to be any rules," complained a lich.

"Exactly," Aldie said. "The rules are all over the place because the essence of being mortal is navigating the Charybdis that is chaos, and the Scylla that is order. Humans have a unique ability to live in both. We Others have only ever had to live in one.

"For us fae, order was our lives. Everything was dictated by our gods. Protocol was paramount. And not just fae—angels, dwarves, gnomes. Our gods demanded order. For other Others, chaos reigned supreme. Dragons, orcs and demons of all manners swam in the unguided pools of their existence. But the human world is something else.

"And so, let me tell you the secret to being mortal. It's knowing when to walk the straight line of order and when to dance the hurricane of chaos. That's it. Figure that out, and you will live the rest of your years happy, secure and joyous."

As Aldie spoke, I saw that he was slowly guiding the crowd out of the conference hall, where the sphinx who had originally taken me backstage was standing. You could tell that she was taking Aldie's new events program in stride. I guess she was embracing the chaos of the situation.

"You haven't seen my hyena and his, ahhh, changeling handler?" I asked.

"Changeling? No. The hyena, however, is tied up outside. We can't have a wild animal running about."

The sphinx was about to launch into a rant about being more responsible with my animals when I saw Egya tied up to a bicycle rack outside.

I ran over to him and hugged the big, hairy lug with all my might. "Oh, thank the GoneGods you're OK."

I looked around, expecting to see Deirdre, but she was nowhere in sight. "Where is she?" I turned to see that Aldie was now outside, the crowd slowly pouring out of the conference hall behind him.

Egya yelped.

"Where is she?" I repeated.

Another yelp.

"Great," I said. "I spend most of my time begging you to shut up, and the one time I need you to speak, you can't."

Egya cackled with genuine mirth.

Bless him ... he'd find a way to laugh being tortured in Hell.

20
DUMPSTERS, DARK ELVES AND PRIVATE PLANES

I unhooked Egya and immediately he grabbed my hand in his mouth, pulling me toward the outside of the conference hall.

"No," I said. "It's too dangerous. Safety in numbers." I nodded toward Aldie and the hodge-podge of adoring Others. "Where do you need that crowd to go?"

Another yelp, and Egya pointed his paw to the corner.

"Aldie," I said, getting the dark elf's attention. I pointed to where Egya had. Aldie nodded in understanding, and we made our incredibly slow progression to behind the hall, where I found Deirdre clutching her chest. She was bleeding, barely conscious, and I suddenly understood what had happened.

Egya and Deirdre were trying to leave when the angel attacked. A fight ensued. The Soul Jar was taken, and when Egya went to find help, the stupid sphinx tied him up.

Deirdre's eyes opened. "Milady. I … I failed you. He has it in his …" A cough cut off her words.

She'd been hurt very badly by that angel. Rage filled me as I went to my friend, helping her to her feet. I don't make many promises, but I made one then and there.

I was going to pay the angel back for what he did.

"Shuush." I wiped her forehead. "No, Deirdre—you did great. We have it. You did great."

If Deirdre heard me, she made no indication of it. Instead, she closed her eyes, her breathing becoming very shallow. I'd been around enough of the dying to know that she wasn't going to make it. Not without help.

↔

"Look here. Another example of mortal chaos," Aldie said. "What do we do when such chaos presents itself?"

The crowd said nothing, and I looked at them with utter disgust. "Seriously. Isn't this obvious? You help her," I screamed, dabbing her wounds with the sleeve of my blouse. Green blood oozed out of the wound in her forehead, and she groaned as her eyes rolled into the back of her head. She was hurting pretty damn bad, and everyone just stood around watching her.

Including Aldie.

Through tears of frustration, I whispered, "You help her. If I had magic, if I could burn time, I'd give whatever I had to help her. I'd burn it all."

"Why?" Aldie asked, still not moving to help.

"Because she doesn't deserve this. She is so good. Better than me."

"Again, why?" There was a tenderness in his voice.

I thought back to everything I'd gone through with Deirdre. All the fights, the talks, the hanging out … She was a royal pain in my ass, and completely oblivious as to how to live in the mortal world, but that didn't stop her from trying. Really trying.

"Once," I said through tear-strained eyes, "she burnt over a month of her life to save three rat pups. No human I know would have even stopped to look at the rats, let alone helped them. Whenever I've needed her, she's been by my side. And whenever she saw an injustice, she was always the first to get involved. The world needs more like her. Not like me. As a vampire, I was selfish and vain. Am no better as a human. And the shit I've done as both an immortal and a mortal automatically makes me ugly."

"Perhaps," Aldie said, putting his hand on Deirdre's forehead. "Perhaps not." The dark elf closed his eyes and whispered a short elvish incantation. The wound on her forehead closed. It didn't wake her up, but at least she was no longer bleeding from that gash. "I give her three minutes of my time," he said.

"And I give her two minutes of mine," the cerberus said, pointing a clawed hand at her.

"Three of mine," announced a troll.

"One of mine."

I watched as, one by one, members of Aldie's crowd sacrificed precious minutes of their lives to save my friend, and as each did so, another wound closed, another bruise disappeared. She was going to make it.

Aldie put a tender hand on my shoulder. "You might not be able to burn time, but that doesn't mean you don't have time to give."

"*Humph,*" I thought, "*more self-help mumbo jumbo.*"

"Perhaps," Aldie said, clearly listening in on my thoughts. "And here's a bit more for you. You spend so much time hating your past that it obscures your future."

"And what should it do?"

If Aldie had an answer to my question, he didn't share it. He just stood next to me as we watched my friend become whole again— minute by burnt minute.

It was quite the tender moment. Then a friggin' angel showed up and ruined it all.

↔

. . .

Oche landed with all the subtlety of a Mack truck slamming into a bicycle, and clearly not getting the memo that bad guys are supposed to soliloquy you with phrases like, "You stole it from me" or "Time to die," opted to pick up a tiny two-door sedan and throw it at Aldie.

Normally Aldie would have tumbled out of the way, but given I was right in front of him and he had dozens of adoring fans standing behind him, he pushed me out of the way of the car.

No way he did that with his natural strength. Aldie was burning time. And not just a minute or two—a feat like that would cost him days, if not weeks.

Tossing the car to one side, he said, "Another piece of mortal chaos. I guess not everyone's a fan."

Oche roared in frustration, pulling out a sword from under his wings. "Shit's about to get real," I muttered in my best Samuel L. Jackson voice before grabbing one of the sedan's fallen hubcaps. Holding it like Captain America's shield, I charged at the hulking beast.

"Kat," Aldie cried out. "What are you doing?"

I could hear the dark elf's footsteps behind mine. *Always my knight in shining armor,* I thought as I drew in close to the angel.

Oche shot the two joints of his wings like fists at my attack. The thing about fighting angels ... because they are overpowered creatures that spent their entire creation obeying orders, they were also predictable. And he was doing exactly what I expected him to do.

I rolled under the winged attack and beneath his feet, where the joint that connected his wings to his back was exposed. Then I thrust the hubcap into that tender piece of flesh as hard as I could. That was their sensitive spot—and hitting him there was the angel's equivalent of getting kicked in the balls (not that I'd know what that was like).

Oche growled in real pain, and then did something I hadn't predicted. He folded his wings inward, wrapping around me with those massive, feather-filled folds. And then he squeezed.

I couldn't breathe. I was literally being smothered by angel wings. *One hell of a way to go,* I thought as I struggled to get out, but as hard as

I did, I couldn't move. I simply wasn't strong enough to push my way out. Not as a lone human.

I was doomed. So, I did the only thing I could. I stopped trying. I conserved my strength and prayed that Aldie would get me out.

21

DARK ELVES AND PRIVATE PLANES

*W*ho said prayers were no longer answered in the GoneGod World? Within seconds I heard a growl— Egya—and a war cry—Aldie. Inch by inch the wings loosened their grip, allowing me to take in precious air, before they unfolded entirely.

Freed, I tumbled out from under Oche and saw Egya and Aldie pulling at one set of wings as the sphinx and two wyverns pulled at another. Three dwarves wrapped themselves around Oche's legs, and a dozen pixies clambered up his back, clawing at his ears, one good eye and his cheeks.

I guess group efforts weren't just for burning time. They were also for overwhelming angels, too.

With all that overwhelming force, I figured it was only a matter of time before Oche would go down. Trouble was, him going down didn't really help our situation. It wasn't exactly like we had rope strong enough to bind him or handcuffs large enough to go around those wrists. We were in a stalemate that could only end with the finality of death.

So be it, I thought.

I grabbed Oche's sword and pointed the tip at his throat. "I don't suppose I could ask you to leave me alone."

"Never," spat Oche.

"Then I see no other way."

"Kat," Aldie said, his voice strained as he wrestled with the angel. "There is no honor in killing a subdued enemy."

"And there is no hope if we leave him alive," I said. "You said that I hate my past. And you were right. Hating my past has only gotten the people I cared for hurt. Maybe I should stop hating the monster I was. Maybe I should embrace her and ask her to help me in moments like these. Maybe that's what this world needs … for me to become the monster I once was."

Closing my eyes, I felt hatred and anger swell within me. I was prepared to kill this angel. I knew it. But more importantly, so did everyone else.

↔

As I prepared to thrust the blade into Oche's neck, I cried out, "Do you not feel my intentions?"

"Who … who are you speaking to?" Aldie asked.

"Him," I said. "The coward standing behind that parked car."

Aldie looked in the direction I had cocked my head and saw Enoch standing there, a forlorn look on his face.

"I do," he rasped.

"And you will do nothing to save him?"

"I cannot. I have run out of tricks. There is nothing I can do."

"So you're content to just watch him die."

"I am," Enoch said, but his tone wasn't even like it usually was. He was in anguish and doing everything he could to hide that from me. But over three hundred years of playing the poker game of life and death, I'd gotten very good at reading others. Enoch was dying inside.

147

"Then I offer you this: a truce. His life for peace."

"I cannot do that," Enoch said.

"You're willing to let him die? For what? A fool's errand."

"Perhaps. But then again, perhaps not. I am willing to let him die for a chance to change everything. He knows my purpose. And he, too, is willing to die."

Shit … I hadn't gambled on that. Still, there was one more thing I could try before slitting an angel's throat. "Then a temporary truce."

Enoch's eyes lit up. "The terms."

"Two weeks."

"I cannot."

"Then one," I said.

"One day?"

"I was going for one week, but OK. Let's regroup for one single day, then we can go right back to trying to kill each other."

Enoch thought this over before nodding. "One day that will start now."

I twisted my wrist so I could see my wristwatch; it was two in the morning. I was getting twenty-two hours out of this deal. That should be enough.

"Very well," I said. "But I get to keep the sword." I lowered my arms and nodded at Aldie.

"Are you sure?"

"He may be insane, but he is honorable. He will adhere to the terms."

Aldie growled, but let go. "The rest of you, I thank you for coming to my aid, but it is time to let the fiend go."

The Others clambered off him. Everyone but Egya, who continued pulling at his wing.

I crouched next to the hyena. "Let him go," I said, petting his neck. "I promise that karma's going to give him his due."

Egya growled as he reluctantly unclenched his jaw.

Freed, Oche jumped several dozen feet into the air before landing next to Enoch. Show-off.

I pointed the sword at the two of them. "One day. Now go."

Without another word, Oche picked up Enoch like he was cradling a child and took to the sky.

We had our truce. Hopefully it was enough time to get to Paradise Lot.

PART VI
INTERMISSION

When Enoch awakens, he is on the basest of planes—Earth. His angel savior is nowhere to be found. The angel did, however, bring the celestial treasure. Something of immense power.

And danger.

The first thing that Enoch must do is find his place on Earth. Establish a base. Garner some followers. Research. Plan.

He knows his mission as clearly as anyone can. Find the gods, and once they are found, uncover the path to them.

But as much as he has purpose, something is wrong—something is missing. For in the deepness of self, Enoch does not recognize who he is.

Once upon a time, he was mortal. Human. This body, these emotions … there should be some sense of familiarity to all this. But there is not. Nothing about who Enoch is today feels right.

It's as if something integral to being human is missing from his very essence.

It takes Enoch months to uncover the problem. He tries everything, but nothing reveals what he knows to be true.

He does uncover it. And like so many great discoveries, it is an accident that leads him to finally understand what has happened to him.

↔

The day Enoch figures it out, he is at a café, mulling over the greatest pieces of the celestial treasure. He knows that in any other context, he should be hiding what is his. That at any moment, marauders could be crashing through the feeble glass windows to get at him.

But this is the GoneGod World, and few can recognize true power anymore. And those who can are too depressed and frightened to seize it. Besides, Enoch is adorned with the Gauntlets of Samson ... bracers that imbue their wearer with incredible strength.

Not even the archangel Michael possesses the strength to beat him.

A young woman comes up to him and says with typical human drollness, "May I take your order?"

Enoch pines for the days when he did not need food or drink to sustain himself. To do so was a matter of pleasure, not necessity. He picks two items from the menu—a soup for its nutritional value and a sandwich with the highest caloric value.

He estimates that the combined items will sustain his body for at least six hours, perhaps longer.

The waitress scuttles off to get his order, and when she returns, she has two soups and two sandwiches. Handing him his order, she delivers the identical items to the table next to him.

The young woman with the same order as him leans over and says, "When I heard what you ordered, I thought to myself, 'That sounds so good.' I couldn't help myself. I hope you don't mind sitting next to a copycat." She giggles at her own joke.

Enoch does not return her mirth—not that she notices. Instead, she turns to her meal, and with a smile too wide for something as base as eating, shovels in the first mouthfuls of food.

With each bite, the gregarious woman makes little noises of pleasure. At first Enoch believes she is acting. But that doesn't make sense. Why put on such drama for something as worthless as lunch?

Going through his briefcase of celestial treasures, he puts in the Eye of Dionysus for the first time since arriving on Earth.

Dionysus was the god of revelry. He was also an insecure drunk whose greatest fear was that the other gods only pretended to enjoy his lavish parties. So he created the lens to ensure that when they cried out in pleasure, it was sincere. Genuine.

When Enoch looks at the world around him through these lenses, he sees humans' true emotions. And this one truly is enjoying her meal.

Looking at himself through the awkward mirror of the metal napkin dispenser, he takes a bite.

He sees no joy in the reflection.

He also sees no disdain.

In truth, he sees no emotion at all.

Is that possible? Humans are contradictions of emotion and logic. And yet his feelings are deeply hampered.

Why?

More importantly, how?

↔

His investigation takes months, but eventually Enoch is able to trace it back to the events of the day the gods left.

It seems that his goal to die was achieved after all. He did die, if only to be brought back by whichever angel entered his chambers. In that second, his soul left his body, but his departure was too late to follow the gods.

And since his savior (not that the mysterious angel saved him at all —more like condemned him) removed him from Heaven, well, it seems that his soul could not follow.

A soul cannot be destroyed. Even the combined powers of all the gods could not do it. So Enoch knows his soul exists, but has no idea where it could be. After all, what does a soul do when it is expelled from one plane of existence into nothing?

It finds another place to exist.

This poses a dilemma for Enoch, for if he is to join the gods, he must not only find them, find a way to them ... he must also find his soul in order to reach them.

Finally understanding the full extent of his problem, he stands, leaving his food uneaten.

22
SELF-HELPING YOUR GOODBYES

*T*he crowd followed us to the airport, a slow procession of Others parading through he street of Okinawa in the middle of the night. It took us almost three hours to get there, and every time I wanted to speed up by, you know, calling an Uber, Aldie reminded me of two things:

One, the private plane section of the airport opened at dawn, so hurrying didn't really matter.

And two: that crowd behind us needed this. They needed the walk, the time to contemplate all that had happened. Time to meditate on their purpose as mortals.

The trouble was, I was also doing some contemplating, and I hated it. I didn't want to be in my head anymore. Evil thoughts swam in its treacherous waters. Thoughts that included regret over not killing Oche. He was a powerful enemy, one that I could have gotten rid of.

So, I did what I always do when I'm stuck in my head. I thought out loud. *"I should have killed him."*

"Perhaps."

"Get out of my head."

"Never," Aldie said with a wink. "But go on. What else are you thinking?"

"OK," I said, figuring that if I was going to be stuck in these thoughts, I might as well have company. "I'm thinking that the Gone-Gods know he deserved it, if for no other reason than because of what he did to Deirdre. She might be OK, but she only survived because of ... well, you. But that was luck. And luck isn't something you can count on in the GoneGod World."

"Perhaps. But then again, perhaps luck and fate and destiny were not lost just because the gods took their magic."

"Spare me the self-help, new-agey crap, will you?"

"Again—never," he chuckled.

"I can feel it," I said, looking at my hands, which only an hour ago wanted to kill a prone angel. "I can feel the monster within me. It's still there and it wants out. It wants to be a part of me again. And what's worrying is that I want it, too. I never had any doubts when it was a part of me. I knew exactly what to do at any given moment. Granted, those moments were filled with guzzling blood and hedonistic bliss ... but they were moments when no uncertainty muddled what I needed to do next."

My brow must have been furrowed with the anguish of the thought, because Aldie, who knew me better than perhaps I knew myself, said, "When I told you that your past blinds you to your future, I was not only speaking of the demon. I was also speaking about the angel."

"What angel?" I said.

"The angel who hunted you for all those years. The angel you eventually killed, but who never truly died."

"Humph, my father and his damned Divine Cherubs."

"That angel hunted you long after you had fully embraced the demon. Even when we were together, years after your father had died, I felt his presence always with us. Embrace the demon, but also embrace the angel within."

"Again—new age, self-help garbage."

"If I had said that to any of them, perhaps. But for you it is quite literal. A demon was a part of you ... but so was an angel, of sorts. You will never truly be complete until you embrace both."

"Sometimes I hate you," I said with a chuckle. "Check that. *A lot* of the time I hate you."

"But now isn't one of those moments," he said.

"Yeah ... now isn't one of those moments."

↔

We got to the airport just before dawn and had to wait thirty frustrating minutes until the first of the staff showed up. He looked confused. Aldie's plane was barely big enough for four people; there were hundreds. But we explained that they were sending us off and the attendant, impressed that we had so many friends, did not let them in.

It was time for Aldie to say goodbye to his adoring fans, something he did in true Aldie fashion. He turned to the lumbering crowd who, in the last two hours, had sacrificed a bit of their time to heal a stranger and thrown themselves into a fight against one hell of an angel. These were the GoneGod World's lost, but as I stared out at the crowd of kitsune, alps and vodniks, dwarves, wondjinas, and pixies, the hodge-podge of Others who had travelled from all over the world to try to better themselves, in their ill-fitting clothes and with their confused looks, I knew I was standing before this world's elite.

An elite who wouldn't be given a chance to shine. There was no time; humans expected them to come ready to fit in and ready to accept their second-class status. Since these folks wouldn't do either, well, let's just say if I had a Magic 8-Ball, it would read: *Outcome looks bleak.*

But whereas I was sure of their bleak future, Aldie hadn't gotten the memo.

"Here's the good news. The GoneGod World is inhospitable, unforgiving. Mean. As the humans say: it fucking sucks. And what's more, the indigenous population sees us as unwanted guests. Refugees who should pack up and go home. They know we can't, and they don't care."

"How is that good news?" I thought, perhaps a bit too loud, because I completely interrupted the flow of Aldie's ... ahem ... rousing speech.

"It is good news, because now we have a chance to prove ourselves. But more importantly, we have a chance to be ourselves. For when the gods allowed us to roam Heaven and Hell, Nirvana and Yomi, Valhalla and Helheim, Elysium and Tartarus, they gave us a home that was ready-made, complete to the specifications of our needs.

"We were children, coddled by gods who ultimately did not really care about us. As proof, they left. But they did not abandon us, for they sent us here to finally prove who we are. *What* we are ... For here we are not creatures of myths and legend. Here we are living, breathing, caring people who share one common goal. We are trying to shape this world not in the image of the heavens we once belonged to, but into a new heaven. A messy, confusing heaven. A heaven that was created for all."

Aldie lifted his hands into the air, and as he did, a flurry of hands, talons, claws and hooves began clapping wildly. "Go forth," Aldie called over the resounding crowd. "Go forth and claim this world. Rebuild your heaven. Find your home."

And with that, the crowd's frenzy worked itself up into an absolute manic state of hooting, howling, yelping and cheering. In the 1960s, I was at *The Ed Sullivan Show* when The Beatles made their first U.S. television appearance, and I was at Woodstock (at least at the night concerts), so I've seen a crowd worked up into unified joy and hope. What Aldie did here was no different.

These Others had hope. More than hope. As long as they carried his words, they had a real chance. Not something I thought possible from a self-help guru, but here we were.

To say I was impressed would have been understating it. I was awed by Aldie and his ability to help. So much so, I could forgive him his tricks. But then he had to go and ruin it by opening his stupid elven mouth. "Don't forget to sign up to our mailing list. Bonus prize: a free seminar on Empowering the Giant Within."

"Yuck."

"What?" he asked. Then, shaking his head. "Never mind. My plane and Paradise Lot await."

23

THE BOY WHO CRIED HYENA AND THE BOY WHO DIDN'T ANSWER

*A*ldie's private plane was surprisingly cramped for such a high-ticket item. Four chairs and a cockpit, with a wee bit of space in the back for luggage. I looked around the tiny cabin, muttering to myself, "Thank the GoneGods I'm tiny."

"What was that, princess? Unhappy with your accommodations? You should try hitching a ride with that valkyrie. She was giving you googly eyes and—"

"No, no … I'm sorry. I don't mean to sound ungrateful. It's just that, I don't know, you've always been Mr. Lavish. I guess I was expecting more."

"The self-help biz doesn't pay as much as you'd think."

"But you have so many fans."

"And most of them can only afford to attend through our scholarship programs, which essentially provides free admission. Then there's booking the theater, the flyers, promos. The only reason I could afford this event was because some strange benefactor paid for everything but my time."

"Enoch, drawing you in."

"Indeed. If I had known that torture was part of the package, I might have negotiated for a retainer."

"And this plane?"

"A gift from a gnome. He's a mechanic in New Jersey, and this old bucket was abandoned long ago. He fixed it up, made it sky worthy and gifted it to me so that I could do what I do."

As he spoke, Deirdre ambled past him, choosing one of the seats. She sat in exhaustion, fumbling with her seatbelt as she did.

She may have been fully healed, but she was still out of it. A changeling warrior needs nature and sunlight to truly heal from any battle, and I knew we needed to get her a mud bath as soon as possible.

Aldie went to help her, guiding the clip in.

"Thank you Son of Leeq."

"Ahhh, you've heard of my father," Aldie said as he finished strapping her in.

"Of course. Every fae has."

"Then you've heard of me?"

Deirdre nodded.

"And ..."

"And ..." Deirdre paused, choosing her next words carefully. "I have learned that legend and truth are not good traveling companions."

"Well said, changeling warrior." Aldie crossed both fists over his chest, a typical fae salute. Of course, it didn't help that it looked exactly like the salute Black Panther did when greeting a fellow Wakandian, but who was I to critique thousands of years of tradition?

Egya put his head on Deirdre's lap and the two of them sat together, waiting for the plane to take off.

"So," I said, cutting into the awkward silence that fell over the cabin, "where's the pilot?"

Aldie shot me one of those devilish smiles of his ... the one he used when he had a real treat in mind. "Why, my dear, you're looking at him."

↔

. . .

"By the GoneGods, no," I said.

"What do you mean, no?"

"I mean *no*. You're the pilot? Do you even have a license?"

Aldie gave me an indignant look before meandering to the cockpit. "Of course." Then he muttered, "The human at the licensing office told me I was very charming when she printed one out for me. Didn't even bother to ask for proof that I'd completed flying school or anything ..."

"What?"

As he sat down, he said, "Calm down and strap yourself in. Or don't ... The truth is, if this plane crashes a seatbelt isn't going to do a damn thing for you."

I expected Aldie to click a few buttons, flip some switches ... You know, the kind of thing you saw in the movies. But he didn't. Instead, he pulled out a clipboard and started writing some things down before pulling out a friggin' compass (and by compass, I mean those medieval devices that help you draw a perfect circle).

"What are you doing?"

"Charting our course," he said without looking up.

I looked at my watch. "How long will that take?"

Aldie looked up at me with genuine confusion. "Kat, you are the human. You know you can't just get in a plane and take off. There are procedures, protocol and whatever 'P' words you humans have to slow things down." He stuck his face back into his clipboard. "For a species that's mortal, you sure have cultivated a lot of ways of wasting time. Now if you don't mind."

"Argh." I sat down in a huff and tried to summon every ounce of patience I had as I counted the hours before Enoch would resume his hunt. Just when I was about to lose my friggin' mind, Aldie clicked a few buttons and I heard a monstrous roar as the engines fired to life. Miracle of miracles—that didn't take too long.

. . .

↔

Turns out we weren't going to be defeated by 'P' words. It was the 'B' in bureaucracy that was going to kill us.

We taxied to the runway, where we sat for hours before we got permission to fly. It seems that airports are real sticklers for booking a take-off time. But that time wasn't completely wasted; I spent half of it watching the seconds tick by as our truce with Enoch was being gradually consumed by airport red-tape. The paranoid monster within me began to wonder if the delay was Enoch's doing.

I mean, he was pretty savvy, but an Other using human red-tape against us made him positively unbeatable. I shook my head. No way an ex-angel who had spent centuries completely detached from the human world could be that cunning ... could he?

The other half of our wait was spent with Aldie sitting crossed-legged on the floor as he spoke to Egya. I couldn't hear what they were saying, but their eyes were locked as Aldie massaged his jaw. Every time I tried to ask what was going on, Aldie would shush me. And Egya would growl in that way dogs did when telling you to back off.

I took the hint and sat in one of the chairs, trying to distract myself from what was to come.

The problem with distracting yourself ... it never works. Especially when you don't have your iPad with *Legally Blonde* pre-loaded on it. So, my mind replayed everything that had happened in the last six months. The fights, my mom showing up, the Soul Jar ... Enoch's obsession with me. I also replayed a strange conversation I had had with an ex-vampire by the name of Lizile. It had happened when my mom showed up and used me to retrieve the Amulet of Souol.

We had traveled to her cabin, where she agreed to give me half of the amulet in exchange for a private chat. My mother had protested, but in the end, it was the only way to get it. And in that conversation, that strange vampire told me something I had dismissed as the ramblings of someone clearly suffering from mortal madness.

She had said I would be instrumental in the war between humans and Others. A war that, according to her, was inevitable.

But there was no war. Not yet, at least. And if you took her words in the context of what the Fates had shown Enoch, there never would be. The world would end before we got a chance to end it for ourselves.

Still, I couldn't shake the feeling that both Enoch and Lizile were right. What if there was a war, and what if that war involved meeting some of the gods? After all, if they left, they could come back.

And since they both had a hard-on for me (well, Enoch at least. Lizile had whatever the female equivalent of a hard-on was ... a clit-on, maybe?), then perhaps I was at the center of something bigger.

I shook my head. *Look at you, Kat. Such a ridiculously huge ego. You're just a human girl with a shit-ton of bad luck. Once this Soul Jar is delivered to Michael, you can go back to Montreal and finally be the normal girl you want to be.*

Normal. What does that even mean? Classes, studying ... boys.

Oh, boys. Like Justin. My heart skipped a beat when I thought of him and all the crap I did to him. He was probably sitting in Montreal, worried that I'd never return. I should call.

Stupid brain, won't let me relax. If I wasn't fretting over the fate of the world, I was fretting over the fate of my relationship.

"Aldie," I said.

"Shuuush."

"Do you have a phone?"

Without looking up, he nodded toward the back of the plane, where a briefcase sat.

"In the case?" I asked.

With a subtle nod, he returned to his humming.

↔

· · ·

In the briefcase sat an old iPhone 5 without a password. I dialed Justin's number and as it rang, I said, "I'll pay you back for the long distance call."

One ring, then two. And as the phone buzzed, I prayed that he didn't answer. I prayed that it would go to voicemail so I could hang up and feel good about having made an effort to reach out.

It wasn't my fault if he didn't pick up, right? It takes two to tango and all that.

But I knew the real reason I was calling was because of what Enoch had shown me in that crystal ball. Justin with someone else—someone not me. A peek into the future, he'd said. And I'd thought it was all a bunch of baloney, but here I was, calling Justin anyway.

It kept ringing. And ringing.

Finally, it did go to voicemail. As soon as I heard Justin's pre-recorded voice, I pulled the phone away from my ear.

I couldn't say what I needed to say over voicemail. I just couldn't.

The old me would have mumbled something about wanting to talk to him, and she would have sounded vaguely penitent without ever saying sorry. The new me just hung up—I would get my chance to do it right when I got back to Montreal—and sat down in my seat.

Or at least I tried to, because as I turned, I was greeted by a very human, very naked Egya. "Hello Kat," he said, not covering up his, well, his ... *his*.

"You're back." I looked past him. "Burnt some time?"

Aldie shook his head. "Nope, the boy did it on his own. I just guided him as he searched for the power to transform."

"What?" I said, my mind reeling with the possibilities. "You still have magic?"

Egya shook his head. "No, I did it without magic."

"How?"

"Aldie. He showed me to channel my inner"—Egya paused, searching for the word—"chi? Chakras? I have no idea; I was never into that kind of stuff."

"Actually, I just helped your breath. It is amazing what you can do if you can just slow the mind, oxygenate the blood and well ... just be."

"Come again?" I said.

"Never mind. The point is that magic isn't just unknown forces being bent to our will. Sometimes magic is our own bodies listening to our needs. Egya here spent centuries being able to transform into a hyena at will. He was forced into that form not because Enoch wanted him to be a hyena, but because that was all Enoch's little trick could pull off. Think about it: if he really wanted to make Egya harmless, he would have turned him into a rabbit or a gerbil. Not a hyena. So, whatever he cast on your friend was designed to unlock something that was already within him. What was once unlocked remains unlocked. And once you open a door—well, doors are designed for you to walk through in both directions."

"Ugh, more self-help platitudes."

"Call it what you want, but through some breathing techniques and guided meditation, I showed Egya how to walk through that door."

"Does that mean he can turn back?" I turned to Egya. "Can you?"

Egya took three deep breaths and said, "I don't know. But I feel different."

"He should. In theory. There are studies that seem to indicate that were-transformation isn't just magic, but rather two states of being in one body. I don't think he'll be able to be fully hyena again, but certainly he can bring out a number of traits. An elongated nose, clawed fingers. Some extra fur to keep himself warm at night. That kind of stuff." Aldie reached into one of his overhead compartments and pulled out a CD. "I did a whole seminar on it. Here's the recording. Very low attendance, unfortunately. I guess were-creatures who are human now weren't really interested in unleashing their inner beasts again. That, or it sounded too far-fetched for them. Whatever it was, that was the talk that made me decide to shift my focus onto Others. There isn't a day that goes by that I'm not thankful for that failure."

"Arrgh. You are too much, Aldie," I said. But even as those words came out, what I really felt was that he wasn't too much, but rather—*something else*. In a good way. A very good way.

Deirdre stirred, and seeing a naked Egya before her, said in a sleepy tone, "Oh good, we're allowed to be naked in public. Finally," before passing out again.

↔

Egya was a good eight inches taller than Aldie and had considerably more bulk that the dark elf, so when he borrowed some clothes, they only wrapped around him, barely concealing anything. He looked like the Incredible Hulk mid-transformation, and I wasn't entirely sure that it was an improvement … especially because Egya was damn hot. Still, at least his bits weren't flapping in the wind anymore.

I gave the stupid chuckler a big hug. "So good to have you back."

"Good to be back."

We lingered there a little too long. I guessed I worried about him more than I'd thought. "I, ahh, should really thank Aldie again. He's put everything at risk and …"

"Awkward hug?" Egya giggled. "Can't express your feelings for too long, Kat … you might finally become that human you want to be." And with that, he chuckled as a giant grin painted his face.

"Here's a feeling I can express," I said, giving him the finger as I walked to the cockpit.

"Thank you," I said to Aldie.

"For?"

"For Egya, for everything."

Aldie did that fists-crisscrossed-on-the-chest thing. "I owe you."

"For what?"

"You know."

"For breaking up with me? That's long gone. Water under the bridge," I lied. It was a wound that hadn't yet completely healed, but with everything that had happened over the past two days, it was starting to.

"No, I do not owe you for breaking up with you. That was necessary for all the reasons I mentioned before. I owe you for *how* I broke up with you. I was unnecessarily cruel."

"Yeah, I'll say." I thought back to that evening. It was a long story, but let us just say that he got engaged to an elf in a very public way on our anniversary.

"I did it that way because I was closing a door."

"Because doors are designed for you to walk both ways through them. Yeah, I've heard."

He nodded. "I needed to close that door. And being cruel was the only way I knew how."

"It's fine."

"Is it?"

"No, but it will be."

"That is enough for now," he said before his brow furled with concern. "That spell Enoch cast on your friend that unlocked his doorway to transformation? Your beast still resides within you. He could use it on you. He could turn you back into a vampire."

"No," I said. "He needs me intact, with my soul in my body. Vampires lose their soul as soon as they're transformed."

"And if he had a spell that would allow you to keep your soul?"

"A vampire with a soul ... who ever heard of that?" I giggled.

Aldie gave me a blank look. He obviously wasn't a Whedon fan. "Whatever he wants or does not want from you ... a spell like the one he used on Egya is powerful magic. Magic that even gods would struggle wielding. You don't know what he is capable of."

"Sadly, I do," I said.

"And ..."

"And I need to get this troublesome thing to the one angel who knows how to deal with him."

"Michael."

"Michael. Now if only we could take off and—"

As if my prayers were answered, the plane's comms came on. We were approved for takeoff.

Yay, now all we needed to do was fly halfway across the world to convince an archangel that we weren't a threat while trying to hand him one of the most powerful magical items on Earth while being hunted by an ex-angel and his henchman.

No problemo...

24

ANGELS AND AIR CONTROL

"*B*ig problemo," I muttered as the plane rattled and shook. After a relatively smooth flight from Okinawa, we were under celestial siege by one enormous and very determined angel.

Oche.

He was flying right next to us, diving in and out of view as he brandished a huge sword in our faces.

I looked at my watch. We still had six hours before the truce ended, and given we were flying over Paradise Lot airspace, that should have given us plenty of time to land and find Michael. But instead, we had an angel riding our ass. "We still have hours left," I yelled.

Aldie shook his head as he held onto the controller, his brow furrowed as he tried to anticipate Oche's next move. "You said one day, right? Since we flew east, we lost hours. Lots of hours. If anything, they gave us extra time."

"Oh, great. Thanks." I was fumbling with Aldie's phone, trying to call Paradise Lot's police station. The thing about phones in the sky is, even though we were closer to the satellites, they don't really work. I guess they were programmed for phones that operated at certain heights. "Can you take us lower?"

"How much lower?"

"I don't know … as low as the highest mountain peak around here?" I studied the screen. "I'll let you know as soon as I get a signal."

"Why?" I heard Deirdre groan with anxiety. "I hate these metal birds. One is meant to ride atop a dragon, not in its belly."

Deirdre was having one hell of a time with it. Egya on the other hand, was laughing.

"What's so funny?" I yelled over my shoulder.

"I just learned how to find my inner hyena—something I have craved since the gods left—and I'm about to die. The gods aren't gone. They're here. And they're fucking with us, laughing their asses off." He pointed to the sky and cackled. "I get the joke, you sadistic bastards. And I love it!"

"Great. We've got Lt. Dan back there."

Aldie groaned. *"Forrest Gump?* The scene on the boat?"

"Indeed."

"Good pop culture reference. Now hold on." Aldie pushed the controller away from him and the plane's nose took a dive. Oche appeared in the descending window. He wore a look of puzzled amusement that said, *Are you crashing the plane for me? How considerate of you.*

"Do we have a signal?" Aldie cried out.

"Planes that are rapidly descending really do make a cartoonish vroom noise," I thought as I stared at the screen. "Nothing yet."

"Keep me posted," he said like he wasn't nosediving a plane into the ground.

"Come on, come on, come on!" I was willing the little 4G symbol to pop up—or 3G, or even a friggin' 'E.' Anything. And just as I was considering searching for a Wi-Fi signal, a single bar of signal appeared. "Got it!"

Aldie pulled on the controller, and we leveled out as I dialed 911. The phone rang. Then rang again.

It rang a third time before I finally heard a soft, lovely voice on the other end say, "Paradise Lot Police Department. Please state your emergency."

"I'm in a crashing plane being chased by an angel because I have Rooh Ina'ah—the Soul Jar, something that the archangel Gabriel told me I needed to deliver to Michael."

Pretty succinct description of our situation, if I do say so myself. But it also sounded insane, and I worried the dispatcher would dismiss me as a prank caller.

Only in Paradise Lot would a statement like that be taken seriously. "OK, I need you to calm down, ma'am, and tell me where you are."

I looked out the cockpit window as a rush of desert rolled before us. "I have no idea. I just see sand. Like I said, I'm in a pl—"

And before I could finish, the plane jolted and I felt a rush of wind. Turning, I saw the sky through the hole that Oche had torn in the back of the plane. And by hole, I mean he ripped off the entire back.

The angel stalked into the cabin, his hand extended. "The Soul Jar."

Deirdre stood. "You shall not pass!"

Did she really just make a Lord of the Rings *reference? She's becoming more and more human every day*, was my last thought as the changeling dove into Oche, forcing him out the back of the plane.

↔

Deirdre was gone, the back of the plane was gone … but what was most worrying was that Egya's cackles were gone. He wasn't laughing, which could only mean one thing.

We were screwed.

Aldie held onto my hand. "You may want to assume the position."

"I thought you said it doesn't do anything."

"It doesn't," he said, hugging his knees.

When in Rome, I thought, and hugged my own.

There were a series of thwacking noises as we hit the ground before bouncing back up and hitting again. We must have done that four times before the windshield broke, inviting in a sandstorm that buried us alive.

25

DESERTS, TREES AND CHOICES

I knew we had survived when I heard Egya's cackle. Normally that noise grated on my recently reinstated soul. But hearing it then was music to my ears. We had survived the crash.

But given that Oche was inevitably waiting for us out there, I knew our situation hadn't improved. As I dug out of the sand that covered my body, I thought of the age-old adage: *Out of the frying pan and into the arms of a murderous angel.*

"You OK?" I asked, reaching out a hand to Aldie.

I couldn't find him. He wasn't there. Moreover, his seat wasn't there. The initial thwacks must have dislodged his seat, which meant that he was somewhere behind us. Thoughts of the worst swam through my head. *"He could be mangled, or buried under sand, suffocating. He could be—"*

"Then we best go find him," Egya said. The were-hyena had already unstrapped himself and was reaching to unstrap my own belt. Say what you will about him, he could be calm in a plane crash. There wasn't anyone else in the world I wanted by my side in a fight.

"OK, let's go." I peeled myself out of my seat and headed to the back of the plane.

Outside, I saw that we had driven head-first into a sand dune.

Desert surrounded us, but because of the nature of the dunes, we had to climb up to see much farther.

We couldn't see any sign of Aldie or Deirdre and Oche. I worried for my fae friends. Aldie for being helplessly ripped out of a plane, and Deirdre because she now faced off against an angel who had bested her in battle before. She was powerful. Very powerful. And for Oche to have done to her what he did showed just how dangerous he was.

"I thought Paradise Lot was an island near Europe," Egya said as we took in the desert's expanse. He pointed in the direction of a single giant oak tree that stood alone in a sea of nothing.

"We are," I said. "I studied this place. Paradise Lot is the only Other-majority place on Earth, with a disproportionate number of portals opening here. Where we are standing was once a lush forest. When the gods left, everything died. And not just died, withered into nothing. Everything but that tree."

"Let me guess, they've nicknamed it the Tree of Life?"

"Good guess." But when I saw his face, I understood that he was playing with me. "You knew that already."

"*Jeopardy.* 1000 points in the 'How Our World Changed' category."

"Humph. Shall we?" I pointed toward the back of the plane. "If we're going to find them, they'll be that way."

↔

There was no point in hiding. Either Deirdre had won and we needed to find her, or she'd lost and Oche would take to the sky, find the wreckage and come after us. All that was left for us to do was find our friends and prepare for a fight.

As we struggled to walk on the uneven sand, I heard Egya breathing hard. He was out of shape, or—

Looking at my friend, I saw that his nose had extended slightly, and the tips of his fingers had elongated into sharp claws. "Shit, Aldie's breathing thing really works?"

175

"It does." His voice came out deeper, sultrier, like a low growl. Egya lifted his nose into the air and sniffed. "Aldie is that way." Another sniff. "And Deirdre is that way." He was pointing in two different directions.

Deciding which way to go was like *Sophie's Choice*—if her choice was deciding which of the two people she loved deeply she was going to save. Truth is, I have no idea what *Sophie's Choice* is about. I've never seen it.

In the end, Egya made the decision for me. "Separating now will only mean we all die. We go for Deirdre. We deal with the threat. And in the unlikely event we survive, we find Aldie." He wasn't laughing, but staring at me with a deadly seriousness I had never seen in him before. He knew the stakes full well, and he was ready to see this to the bitter end.

We trekked in the direction of where Deirdre should be. It took about ten minutes of walking, but eventually we found her. She was fine, walking in the direction of the tree.

"Deirdre," I called out, running to my changeling friend. "Deirdre!"

The changeling turned and let out the biggest yelp of joy. "Milady! Milady lives. I was sure you were consumed by the demise of the flying beast."

Tears of relief poured out of her and she wrapped one powerful arm around me. It was only up-close that I saw her other arm hung useless at her side. "Your arm?"

"Destroyed in the crash."

"What do you mean, destroyed? I'm sure it's only broken. A cast and some time and you'll be good as new." But as I took a closer look, I knew I was lying. Her arm was mush. It must have broken in two dozen places. The fact that she wasn't reeling in pain was a testament to the changeling's strength.

Tear of remorse flowed from me. "I'm so sorry," I said. "I'm so sorry for bringing you into this. I'm so sorry—"

"No, milady. I am grateful, for you have given me something that I craved more than life itself. Purpose."

"Purpose?"

She nodded. "And right now, my purpose is to prepare for the angel's return."

Wiping away tears of my own, I looked around. "Where ... where is he?"

"Mid-battle, I heard a ringing. The brutish angel took to the sky before stating that he would return to finally end me. I can only assume his master called him, and that the two of them will return imminently. I am going to the tree, as it is the only place with even ground and cover. It is the best place for us to stage our final stand."

"Final stand, eh?" Egya giggled. "Optimistic much?"

Deirdre gave Egya a look that would have silenced a banshee. "Yes, our final stand. For today we die. Let it be glorious."

26

ANGELS, STONES AND
INDECISIONS

*T*he tree was massive, with a low canopy hanging just above us. If I jumped, I could grab one of the low-hanging branches, but I saw no strategic advantage to it. The only thing this tree really offered us was cover, which took away Oche's ability to use his flight against us.

Deirdre was right: we were doomed. We were a weaponless, five-arm-strong adventuring party about to storm the gates of Mordor. Or rather, the gates of Mordor were about to storm us.

I really wished Aldie was with us. His elven prowess was sorely missed. But more than that, I found myself craving one of his *believe in yourself* speeches. I could really use a pep talk.

Deirdre and Egya were hard at work gathering stones. They were counting on the David vs. Goliath win ... I, on the other hand, was less optimistic that a well-aimed rock would turn the tide of this battle.

But if Aldie had taught me anything, it was that if you believed you were doomed, you probably were. Especially considering the only other thing that would save us—the phone I had used to call 911—was somewhere among the destruction of the plane we'd just crashed in.

So, stones it was.

We must have built about three decent-sized piles when Egya lifted his nose to the air and said, "They're here."

Oh yay!

↔

Stepping out from under the canopy, I watched as Oche lowered from the sky, Enoch cradled in his arms like they were newlyweds. Hah—newlyweds. I wondered what my death would do to our honeymoon. Knowing Enoch, he probably had some zombie spell in his arsenal and his revised plan was to reanimate me, *Walking Dead* style.

Still, I had one ace up my sleeve.

"Still want this?" I held up the Soul Jar.

Enoch nodded. "I'm afraid, dear Katrina, that we are past bartering for your life or the lives of your friends. This is the end game for you."

"I know," I said. "I figure that I'm doomed, Fates predicting our nuptials or not. Still, just because you're over me doesn't mean I can't hurt you."

"You cannot," he rasped.

"Oh, but I can." I set the Soul Jar on the ground and, picking up a large rock before me, I held it over the tiny magic item. As soon as I did, Oche tensed as he prepared to rush at me.

Enoch held out a steadying hand. "Humph—do you really think an item as powerful as the Soul Jar can be destroyed by a mortal hand and an ordinary rock?"

"I have no idea, but from the way you just stopped your pet pigeon, I'm taking it that you don't, either."

Enoch may have been an expert poker player, but even the best at hiding their telltale signs will break when something they truly love or need is threatened. Enoch's eyes twitched. That was all I needed to know that he wasn't willing to risk it.

Besides, I knew I was right the minute I looked at him. I was wearing his little lens—the Eye of Borvo—and it revealed his greatest desires. Whereas when he landed his desires were a mixture of killing us and getting the Soul Jar, as soon as I threatened it, his desire became very much about stopping me.

"So, what's it going to be?" I said. "Let them go?"

He tilted his head. "You still fight for them."

"Always."

"And if I do ... the Jar?"

"No," I said. "I'll never give you this. Never."

"So then, what leverage do you have?"

"An appeal to your humanity. That is all I have left. I ask you to find the kindness and decency that still thrives in your soul and let them go."

Something that I said clearly touched a nerve, because Enoch hesitated. There were no "It's too late" or "I have a greater purpose" speeches. He considered my plea.

"I so wish I could, but I have gone too far down the path of wrong to change now. But you know that. Just as you know that this little banter won't change anything."

"I know," I said.

"Then what is the purpose of all this?"

"Egya," I said, "any good news?"

There was a pause and a sniff. "Yes. A minute, maybe a bit more."

"The purpose," I said, staring down Enoch with rage-filled hate, "was to stall you while we waited for the cavalry to arrive."

Egya's new super-nose was wrong; we didn't have to wait a minute. We only had to wait another three seconds before the earth shook with a deafening voice.

"What is the meaning of all this?" thundered the archangel Michael as he hovered above us. I didn't think there was an angel in this world or any other that could be bigger than Oche, and I was wrong. Michael was. Not by much, but there was a bulk there that Oche didn't have.

And stature. Put the two of them side by side and you knew who was in charge.

Next to Michael hovered another angel I had never seen before. She was slender, tall and looked like a young Cindy Crawford—if that was, Cindy was brandishing a glowing sword.

"Ahh, Miral and Michael have joined the party. Archangel and Leader of the Celestial Army, I welcome you," Enoch rasped. "But this affair is not to be attended by two as lowly as you. This affair demands higher beings with a larger grasp of universal needs."

"Holy guacamole, did he just imply that the archangel Michael is a lower being than his human ass?"

Egya howled with inhuman laughter as Deirdre tried to shush the half-turned hyena, or boy, or whatever the hell he was now. Damn, I must have thought that one out loud.

"Silence, AlwaysMortals," Enoch growled. "None of you truly grasps what is at play here. If you think these two angels will do anything to change the outcome of this day, you are laboring under a severe misapprehension."

I lifted a confused eyebrow. "That's a convoluted way of saying they're not going to help? But to your point, I don't know about that. It's all pretty simple, really. You've got a hard-on for this and me."

He let out a dismissive breath.

"Oh, come on," I said. "You're honestly telling me that if I had a change of heart and were to welcome you into my oh-so-pretty bosom, you'd say no?" I puffed up my chest to give him a better view of my, um, assets. "The answer is still, 'Even if you were the last man on earth,' by the way. Anyhoo ... you want this and you want to end it all."

I picked the Soul Jar up and held it up high. "Gabriel told me to give you this."

Michael narrowed his eyes as he stared at the tiny, seemingly innocuous pendant in my hands. As soon as he realized what I held, I swear to the GoneGods electricity coursed through his eyes, causing the tiny hairs on my body to stand up and demand I run.

But I didn't. I held my ground. "He said you will protect the world from the evil that would seek to use this to their own, private gain. That you were the only guardian left in this world or any other who knew what to do with this. That the hierarchy of order is yours to uphold." As I spoke the words, I couldn't remember Gabriel saying any of that stuff, and yet the words flowed out of me like they were the only truth I was allowed to speak.

Holy ghost, Batman, I thought, *I'm being used as a celestial mouthpiece.*

And that pissed me off. I hate being used. By people, other ex-vampires and angels ... I'm not their toy to be manipulated. I shook my head and summoned my own will to speak. "I don't know about all that. What I do know is that this asshole wants it. And let me repeat, just in case you missed it: Enoch here is planning on ending all life after he gets it."

Enoch looked up at the angels. "Miral, Michael—leave. I am here doing God's will."

"And what is His will, exactly?" Miral pointed the tip of her sword at Enoch.

As soon as she did, Oche took a step, shielding Enoch from her should she choose to swoop down and smite his raspy ass.

"Do you threaten the Witness?" Oche snarled.

"Silence, lowly angel," Miral shot back.

Oche pulled out his own sword in answer. "I am no longer one of your minions to command. I serve a higher purpose now. I serve him."

"A human?"

"The Witness."

Michael lifted an ominous hand, and in a voice that could have sent the Kraken back to the deep to think about what it did, said, "Enough. Let the Witness speak."

Enoch nodded. "Thank you, archangel. I have witnessed the gods leaving centuries before they did, and I have scoured this universe and others in search of their reasoning. I have come to one undeniable conclusion: They left—*He* left—because we were not worthy of His love. Thus, we must prove our worth by sacrificing all to find Him again. That is my purpose, and has been since the day I learned of His plans."

"Yeah, yeah ... Except Mr. I-Shouldn't-Have-Smoked-a-Pack-a-Day over here thinks he's the only one worthy to do so, and plans on killing the rest of us first, then using our dead bodies as a ladder to get to where He went."

Michael pursed his lips, like he was debating who he should kill, before saying, "Traversing universes requires the Power of Will." The way he said that made me think he wasn't pulling a phrase out of Aldie's self-help seminars. The Power of Will was a thing ... a thing that Michael understood.

Looking up at the angel, I was beginning to wonder if he was going to help. He looked as though he understood Enoch's words, that on some level they resonated with him. From the way things were going, I was beginning to think those two might just flap their wings and fly away.

"No," I growled. "Whatever reason the gods have for leaving doesn't give you the right to kill us all so you get a ticket out of here. You're in the muck of it with us.

"And you." I pointed at Michael. "I can't believe you are even entertaining this guy. Seriously? Gabriel told me that you were one of the good guys. Seems like he was the one laboring under a misapprehension. Gabriel literally died to get this. And what do you do? Deliberate? Contemplate? I don't think I should give this to you anymore. I don't think this thing should exist. For the life of everyone, I'm done with the bullshit."

I slammed the jar onto the ground and brought down the stone with the fury of everything in my own soul.

27

CLASH OF THE ANGELS

*T*ime slowed. I guessed it was another one of Enoch's tricks. I watched as my hand that should have smashed into the jar in a millisecond ebb its way down to the ground with frustrating slowness. My mind was operating at normal speed, though.

I heard Michael's voice. "Do not do that."

"I will do whatever it takes to protect this world from creeps like you," I said. Evidently my mouth was operating at normal speed, too.

So, this wasn't one of Enoch's tricks. It was Michael. The archangel was burning time to stop me from destroying the damn thing. "What is it that you want?"

"I already told you, and I'm not in the habit of repeating myself. Well, actually I am, but not here and not now." Michael clearly wanted me to not smash the thing, but given that he didn't swoop down and stop me, I knew he couldn't. His only hope was convincing me to stop.

I wasn't going to stop. And seeing my hand inching its way toward the jar only served to frustrate me all the more. "He orchestrated all of this. The gods rising, the jar being freed from the museum and Yomi ... all of it was his plan. But you know, I could have forgiven him all that. Enoch was doing everything that he thought he should do. I get that. So, I'm going to destroy this thing because of Harry."

"Harry?"

"While going through all the shit I had to go through to get this, I met this yeti—Harry. He was a wonderful being. Pure, beautiful. Kind. Funny in that dorky kind of way. And now he's gone because of this. I just keep thinking about him and how he didn't need to die. So, if you want the truth, I'm destroying this because I don't want any more Harrys to die."

"Even so, that Jar could be the answer to so much," Michael said.

"Like what? More jerks like him causing carnage and mayhem to get it? No, I'm done. This thing goes. Now." I tried to will my hand to come down faster.

"And what of Gabriel's sacrifice? He did everything he could to free it from its prison."

That gave me pause. Gabriel had done so much, given up so much just to get this thing out. Why?

"OK, I'm listening. Why?"

"I do not know, but I can hazard one guess. Immortality has been denied us all, Others and humans alike. When an Other dies, we cease to be. But when a human dies, its soul is lost to the ether of nothing. With the Soul Jar existing here, in this realm of being, the souls of all who die from this point forward can be gathered in one place."

"For what purpose?"

"I do not know," Michael thundered, his frustration palpable. "Perhaps Gabriel holds out hope that a heaven may be reopened for the human souls to find life everlasting."

"Or assholes like him could use it to destroy us. I mean, he clearly wants this for the Power of Will. What is that, anyway?"

Michael folded his arms. "Something not for mortal knowledge."

"OK. Then bye bye, Jar."

I could feel Michael's deliberation before he let out an audible sigh that sounded like a jet engine powering down. "The heavens and hells were controlled by the Power of Will. Human souls were what allowed those domains to exist."

I thought about my own time in Yomi and how I could bend things to my will. In there I was uber powerful, able to manipulate reality as I pleased. "The Power of Will. It is our human souls that allow it all to be, isn't it?"

"Yes."

"You know, that makes your arrogance about how we humans are sub-beings kind of cheeky, given what our souls can do."

"Indeed."

"I'm still not convinced anyone should have access to such abilities," I said, my hand continuing its course.

"I must admit that I agree. Still, my brother would not have sacrificed his life if he did not believe we needed such things. I swear to you that I will protect the Soul Jar."

"And how do I know you won't use it for your shit?"

Michael thought about that for what felt like an eternity, especially given that my hand was only a couple inches above the jar, before saying, "Dear mortal, my oath to you is this: I will not use the power held within without your permission. From this moment forward, you shall be the only key that will unlock its abilities."

I knew Others didn't make oaths lightly. In fact, they only ever agreed to oaths if they felt certain they could fulfill them—or would die trying. And this was the archangel Michael making the oath, which gave it even more gravity. "In other words, I have to give you permission?"

"Yes."

"And you won't pull some Other shit by saying that you want to use it for one purpose while hiding another purpose in the fine print?"

"I will speak plainly to you. Always."

"And should I die?"

"The Soul Jar will be locked away forever."

"And should you die?"

He scoffed at this.

"Hey," I said, "we're all mortal now."

"Indeed. There are … other angels who will uphold my oath in my absence."

"Like Miral there."

"She is chief amongst them, but she is not the only one."

I looked up at Michael. I was still wearing the Eye of Borvo, which meant that I could see his true desire. And in that moment, I saw an angel who desired two things: to honor his dead brother and to keep his oath to me.

He was going to do exactly what he promised, which meant I got the final say on the whole thing. Not sure I liked the responsibility, but I thought about all the danger and death that came of getting this out. If Gabriel saw a purpose in smuggling this thing out, that purpose had yet to reveal itself.

But whatever he saw coming was important. It must have been.

I thought about Harry and the others who had died for this thing. Their sacrifice needed to mean something. It had to.

"OK," I said. "I accept."

Time regained its normalcy as the stone hit the ground next to the Soul Jar with an unsatisfying thud.

↔

As soon as time was back to normal, three things happened. The first was Oche taking to the sky, wings and arms outstretched as he grabbed both Michael and Miral, pushing them up and into the clouds. He was buying Enoch time.

Time that the raspy man used to pull out a clock that only the GoneGods knew what it did—teleport, make him invisible, keep him warm and toasty? Rocks came flying over my head as Egya and Deirdre threw them at Enoch to stop him from getting to me. Seems Egya's pile of rocks was a good idea after all.

Two stones hit him in the forehead, knocking him down. I snatched up the Soul Jar and ran back to my friends. If he wanted this, he'd have to take on the three of us.

But Enoch didn't. Instead, he turned over and started coughing red blood onto the dry, sandy ground beneath him. "No, no, no." He slammed his fist on the ground. "I do not deserve this. I do not deserve to die like this!"

"Cancer," I muttered.

The word cut through his rage like a knife. Looking at me through bloodshot eyes, he cried out, "I served them with all my being. I gave them everything! And they left me here to die, not from old age or natural causes, but from that cursed disease growing within me now."

He was crying, but did not move. He was too weak to do that. He had given everything to get to this point, and it wasn't enough. He knew that. We all did.

Michael dropped down to the ground and landed by Enoch's side, cradling the former archangel in his arms. Looking up, I saw Oche and Miral fighting, and from the way they tussled, it wasn't clear which one would win.

Still, Michael had disengaged to be by Enoch's side.

"Why, Michael?" Enoch rasped. "Why was He so cruel?"

"He was not," Michael said with a gentleness I did not think his overbearing stature would allow. Looking at me, he said, "Bearer of the Soul Jar, will you allow me to return this man's soul so that he may be whole?"

So, here was my first decision to make. Let Enoch have his soul back. With all the horror he had caused, I wasn't sure he deserved it. Then I felt a gentle hand on shoulder. "Everyone deserves to be whole," Egya said.

I turned and looked him in the eyes. He was back to his human self now. Next to him stood Deirdre, cradling her arm. She nodded in agreement.

If the two of them could forgive Enoch enough to return his soul, then so could I.

Walking over, I handed Michael the jar. "Don't make me regret this."

The archangel nodded before putting two delicate fingers over the jar's opening. The mouth opened just wide enough for his massive fingers—like it was always that large an opening.

Michael's fingers rested inside for a moment before he pulled out Enoch's soul like he was teasing out a delicate thread from an intricate quilt. Unlike other souls, which have a silvery, off-white effervescent glow to them, Enoch's was pure white. "God asked me to find a human worthy to serve him," Michael said as he held Enoch's soul. The white energy bustled like it was trying to escape. "And I searched for that human. I did not only search the present, but went to Father Time, asking the old man to help me search *all* times.

"In all time, amongst all the humans born and to be born, I only found one soul truly good enough to serve. One." The white energy grew more frantic, unstable. Looking closer at Michael's hand, I saw flakes of angelic skin burn off as several pustules swelled, threating to burst. The soul was scorching his hand, not that the archangel gave any sign he was in pain. "One—yours!"

Michael's voice boomed that last word like the Punisher does when he's about to do something particularly nasty and vengeful.

"So, God sought to test my choice. It was not an accident that Oche fell upon your home. It was no coincidence that the Nephilim happened upon you when tending to the dead. It was one last test, all to see if this"—he held Enoch's soul up—"was worthy of Him."

Without another word, Michael brought down the soul on Enoch. He was reuniting the man with what he had lost and, because I'm human and use my mouth to eat, I figured that was the orifice he'd use to get the soul into him.

But Michael didn't place the soul in Enoch's mouth. He poured it through the man's eyes. With screaming rage, Enoch's soul seeped back into the human. "You think the gods left you behind as a punishment," Michael boomed. "After eons of divinity, you are still a limited mortal, confused by their ways. The gods did not leave you behind because they were displeased with you. They left you behind as a reward. A final release from servitude. A second chance to live your life as was intended. Mortal, human and complete."

The man stopped struggling. Once the light was fully absorbed, he sat on his knees, his head down as human tears dripped on the hot concrete before him.

"Your soul was their parting gift, Enoch. And my only hope for you is that now that you are complete, you will finally understand."

Enoch, now whole, burst into tears and wails of unbearable pain.

Oche dropped from the sky to be by his master's side. "What did you do?"

"What I had to," Michael answered.

"No. No, he does not deserve this anguish. He is the best of us all." And with tear-laden eyes, he looked at me. "You ... you did this."

With speed beyond anything I had known possible, Oche picked up the stone that I had intended to use to destroy the jar and threw it at me.

Right at my head.

28
GOODBYE MY LOVERS

*W*hen I woke up, I was in a hospital bed. There was an angel standing over me. As in a literal angel.

"Am I dead?" I asked.

"Stop being so dramatic, girl," a familiar voice said. "You're just waking up from a coma."

"A long one," the angel said and as soon as I heard her voice I realized who I was looking at. Miral … the angel from the battle. Of course, now she looked different, having traded her sword for a stethoscope.

"What … what happeend?"

"Oche hit you in the head with a rock," Egya said, taking my hand in his. "Good shot. Something that would have killed you if it wasn't for Miral here, you'd be dead."

"Did you..?" I touched my head. There were bandaids wrapped around my skull and it was tender to the touch.

Miral nodded. "Not much. Just enough to keep you alive. The rest was up to your natural healing abilities. You're not out of the woods yet," she was testing my blood pressure as she spoke. "You'll need bed rest for a few days, but you'll be on your feet in no time."

"How long was I out?" I asked.

No one answered, which was troubling enough. But when even Egya didn't have a witty quip, that's when I really started to worry.

"How long?" I repeated.

"Four weeks," Miral finally said.

"Four weeks? That means that—"

"Valentine's is just around the corner," Egya chuckled.

I smiled at the Ghanian. *'Thank the GoneGods ... he was still annoying.'*

↔

I spent the next three days in bed, catching up on everything that happened. I had been knocked out. Oche and Enoch, seeing that they had lost, surrendered the Soul Jar over to Michael.

And I had been playing Sleeping Beauty for the last few weeks with Egya, Aldie and Deirdre refusing to leave my side.

Friends to the end.

On my last day in the hospital, I got a visitor ... someone I had been expecting for some time now.

Michael hunched over as he entered my hospital room and stared at me with overbearing silence.

"I suppose you want to know my story?"

He shook his head. "The annoying hyena man told me all."

"So why are you here?" I asked.

"To thank you."

"For what?"

"For honoring my brother's wishes," he said with a deadly seriousness.

"Yeah, Gabriel was a good guy."

"And a fool," Michael said, nodding.

"I don't know about that. If he was a fool, then aren't we all? After all, you really do believe that the gods abandoning the Others on Earth was a gift?"

Michael sighed, looked around the room for a place to sit and not seeing one, resigned himself to standing before he finally said, "I have to. I have seen the face of good. Served Him with every fiber of my being. I have to believe that this," gestures around him, "is either my reward or one more way to serve. Perhaps both."

"You're pretty naïve for you age."

Michael looks down at me and at first I thought I had pissed him off. Again. Then he bellowed out in laughter, sending thumbing reverberating base through me, "Perhaps. But the naïve part of me is also the happy part of me."

"Always look at the bright side of your life," I hummed.

"Excuse me?"

"Not a Monty Python fan? Nevermind then ... what's the not so happy part?" but if Michael had an answer he didn't share it. Instead, he said, "Enoch is dying. Cancer. I now understand why he is so bitter."

"We're all dying, Michael," I said. "Some of us faster than others ... but we're all dust in the end."

"As it was intended to be."

"Sure," I agreed. "If that floats your boat, then, yeah ... as it was intended to be."

↔

We went to the airport later that day. Aldie was already there, with a ticket to Melbourne in his hand. "My next seminar," he said, shyly.

I gave my ex a big hug and a kiss on the cheek. "Thank you. For everything."

"All part of my purpose," he said, before snapping his fingers twice and adding, "You really should attend one of our weekend getaway seminars. The next one is on how to embrace your mythical past and use it to help mold your epic future. We have a ton of inspirational speakers: Johnny Appleseed, Paul Bunyon, the Jolly Green Giant. And, oh! the minotaur that guarded Minos' Labyrinth will give the keynote on how he turned his legendary riddles into the world's leading Escape Room experience. He made a mint riding that wave. So, you in?"

He gave me that look of his ... the one that says there's always a good reason for everything, even drowning in lava. *'At least you'd be warm,'* I thought.

"Excuse me?" he said, confusion on his face.

"Never mind." I shook my head. "You're just ..." I looked deep into his impossibly blue eyes and sighed. Why fight it? "You're just rubbing off on me."

"So, you'll come?"

"Maybe. I'll come to one of your events. Eventually."

"Excellent." He clicked his heels like Dorothy ruby-slippering her way home, and taking my arm, helped me onto the tram. "I'll put you on our mailing list. Lots of value-add content in there. Lots."

"I'm sure," I said, stopping before security. Then, turning around, I gave him one more goodbye kiss, this one on the lips. "Thank you, Aldie. You are ..." I searched for the words until I found the perfect ones. "You just are."

His expression lit up with a smile that threatened to split his face in two. "Thank you, Katrina. That is truly a great compliment, coming from you."

29

HELLO MY LOVER

*E*gya, Deirdre and I returned to Montreal by coach, and what I was praying would be a normal life. We started our journey in first class, continued it in a private plane and, now that it was over, it felt right to fly home in the style that most people do. I'm not saying that first-class flights and private planes are bad, but if the people who have that kind of luxury go through the kind of shit we just went through on a regular basis, then give me economy class any day of the week.

Back home, we hired a taxi and made our way to campus. Egya and Deirdre walked up to the dorm, but I wanted a few minutes to myself. I needed a walk to clear my head and think about things. It was, after all, February 14th. I might have missed the first few weeks of school, but I had made it back in time for Valentine's. *Surprise, Justin!*

Oh Justin ... How I looked forward to seeing him and making my return his best Valentine's ever—if you catch my oh-so-not-subtle-at-all drift. I could just see our reunion now. He'd say, "Kat, where have you been?" and I'd be all like, "Miss me, lover?" and he'd take me into his arms and everything would be OK. We'd make whoopee, as Ella puts it, and then I'd tell him everything. Everything, and we could roll the credits on our fairytale romance with the classic *And they lived happily ever after* clause.

Wishful thinking, I know, but I kind of felt like I deserved it. I had just saved the world ... *twice*.

Off in the distance, a flock of birds was flying and diving and gliding in a manner that reminded me of Alfred Hitchcock's' classic horror, *The Birds*. And me, being me, I went over to investigate closer.

As I did, I continued to think about Justin and what the future had in store for us. I really wanted things to work out, but fairytale endings were few and far between in the GoneGod World. We'd most likely fight, and maybe worse.

Whatever our end, the last thing I expected was to see Justin holding another woman while fighting a flock of metal birds that circled the campus above.

What the hell did I miss here?

ALSO BY RAMY VANCE

Mortality Bites Series

Mortality Bites

Family Matters

Superhero Me!

Orphaned Follies

Dawn of a Thousand Sunsets

Three Dead Gods

Run, Kat, Run

Encantado Dreams

The Heaviest of Burdens

Looking for a great deal? Grab these book bundles...

Setting Fires with Dragons - complete series

Mortality Bound - complete series

GoneGod World - Complete series

Series Starter - Bundle

ALSO BY RAMY VANCE

Mortality Bites Series

Mortality Bites

Family Matters

Superhero Me!

Orphaned Follies

Dawn of a Thousand Sunsets

Three Dead Gods

Run, Kat, Run

Encantado Dreams

The Heaviest of Burdens

Shattered Vows

GoneGod World Series

GoneGod World

Keep Evolving

CrystalDreams

Penemue's Inferno

Looking for a great deal? Grab these book bundles...

Setting Fires with Dragons - complete series

Mortality Bites - complete series

Mortality Bound - Complete series

Series Starter - Bundle